When the Power of Love Reaches Across Time

Christmas Past

ROBERT VAUGHAN

THOMAS NELSON PUBLISHERS®
Nashville

A Division of Thomas Nelson, Inc.
www.ThomasNelson.com

This book is for
Jenny Baumgartner

Published in Nashville, Tennessee, by Thomas Nelson, Inc.

This is a work of fiction. The characters, incidents, and dialogues are products of the author's imagination and are not to be construed as real. Any resemblance to actual events or persons, living or dead, is entirely coincidental.

Scriptures are from the KING JAMES VERSION of the Bible.

Library of Congress Cataloging-in-Publication Data

Vaughan, Robert, 1937-
  Christmas past : when the power of love reaches across time / Robert Vaughan.
    p. cm.
  ISBN 0-7852-6235-0 (hardcover)
  I. Title.
  PS3572.A93 C48 2003
  813'.54--dc21   2003012679

Printed in the United States of America
1 2 3 4 5 — 05 04 03

One

Timothy Jerome Carmichael had been called "T. J." for his entire life, and somehow it still suited him as a grown man of thirty-nine. His office at 21 Music Square West overlooked the RCA Building in downtown Nashville. Richly paneled and tastefully decorated, the suite reflected T. J.'s status as one of the most successful artists' representatives in the music business, who traveled frequently to scout new talent around the country and make deals in New York and L.A.

T. J. held the phone away from his ear, drumming his fingers impatiently on the desk.

"Thank your for holding Mr. Carmichael. Mr. Douglas will be right with you."

As T. J. continued to hold, an advertising brochure on his desk caught his eye. Bright-red letters spelled "*Christmas Past*," the title accented with boughs of holly. The cover featured a picture of a beautifully restored antebellum house, its great, white Corinthian columns laden with greenery and a Christmas wreath hanging from the front door.

"T. J.!" An effusively friendly voice boomed through the receiver and broke into T. J.'s rare daydreaming. "Thanks for waiting. How are things going? Did you have a nice Thanksgiving?"

T. J. cast the brochure aside. "Very nice. Ate too much."

"That's what Thanksgiving is all about, isn't it? That and football?"

"Yeah, well, I'm sure it's more than that. So, have you made a decision about Corey Doolin?"

"I'm told you have an offer on the table from ABC. Is that true, or is this just your way of giving me a little poke?"

"Listen, I'd poke you with a cattle prod if I thought it would help. You're not surprised that ABC has made an offer, are you? Corey is the hottest property in the country right now. So, where does HeartNet stand?"

"You might say that we are engaged in serious discussion at the moment."

"Okay, let me give you a little something to discuss. Corey's 'Christmas Past' is number three, 'Waiting for You' is number five, and 'Ruby Lips,' which has been on the charts for forty-two weeks, is still in the top ten, at number seven."

"But you're talking *country*," said Evan.

"Is there any other music chart?" T. J. asked, chuckling.

"Look, Heartland Network emanates from Nashville. And when you say Nashville, the first thing people think about is country music."

"What's wrong with that? Seems to me that would make a Corey Doolin special a natural."

"You're preaching to the choir, T. J. But there are a few people here at the network who are afraid that a country music special would just reiterate our Nashville connection."

"And why would that be a bad thing? Are you ashamed to be based in Nashville?"

"Come on, T. J., you know better than that. We aren't turning our back on country music, but we want people to know that HeartNet is more than that. We know we have the pickup truck and feed-store-hat crowd, but we also want to reach the ones who drive BMWs and wear Gucci."

"You sound like my wife."

"I'll take that as a compliment. Madison is one of our brightest stars, and we're lucky to have her," Evan said. "Come to think of it, so are you."

"So I'm told." T. J. looked at his watch.

"Listen, T. J., give me just a little more time to bring the others around. It's getting very close to Christmas, and you've been in the business long enough to know that not much gets done during the Christmas season."

"That's true, but remember that offer from ABC."

"What is the offer?"

"I'm sorry, I can't tell you that. It's generous, but I wouldn't call it preemptive. If you want to be in the game—"

"If I can get everyone on board, and I think I can, we'll top ABC's offer. I promise you that. Is that worth keeping them at bay for a few more days?"

"I can hold them off until after Christmas," T. J. agreed.

"Are you staying in town for the holidays? Just in case I need to get ahold of you?"

T. J. picked up the brochure that had somehow appeared on his desk and looked at it for a moment before he answered. "I'm not sure where I'll be for Christmas. But you can always reach me on my cell."

"Good, then I'll stay in touch," Evan promised.

"If I don't talk to you again, Merry Christmas!"

"Merry Christmas to you."

T. J. hung up the phone, then opened the advertising piece to read the copy inside.

**Experience the joy of our Savior's birth
without the distractions of modern life.
Come join us for a peaceful, Victorian-era Christmas Past
at Gracehall. We are located twelve miles from
Possum Hollow on County Road 4,
in the Great Smoky Mountains.**

As a child, T. J. Carmichael had accepted Jesus as his Savior. He and Madison were married in a Christian church, and the kids were enrolled in a Christian school. But T. J. couldn't remember the last time he had been to Sunday service.

The phone buzzed. "Yes?"

"Corey Doolin on line one," said his secretary.

"Thanks, Linda." T. J. punched the glowing button. "Corey, how's the voice?"

"How's my voice? I could have two broken arms and two broken legs, and you wouldn't even notice."

"Do you?"

"What if I did?"

"I'd still ask how's the voice."

Corey laughed. "All right, all right—at least I know where I stand. So, what's the latest?"

"How does 'An Evening with Corey Doolin' sound? You'll sing a half dozen songs, introduce a few guest artists—who, incidentally, will owe you big-time for the exposure—and do it all in a one-hour, prime-time television special."

"Have we got the deal?" Corey asked excitedly.

"We've got an offer from ABC," T. J. said. "But I'm also talking to the Heartland Network. I think we can do even better with them, so I don't want to commit to ABC just yet."

"You're the man. I leave all that stuff to you."

"Good. You keep that attitude, and you'll go far in this business. What are you doing for Christmas?"

"I'm going to the Bahamas. What about you?"

"I don't know yet. Wait." T. J. picked up the brochure. "Did you send me this flyer about a Christmas Past?"

"A flyer on 'Christmas Past'?"

"No, no, this has nothing to do with your song."

"Then what is it?"

"It appears to be a kind of bed-and-breakfast called Gracehall, where they celebrate a Victorian-style Christmas. I just wondered if you sent it, because of the name."

"Never heard of it. You think we ought to sue them or something?"

"Why would we do that?"

"Well, they're using the same title."

"If we did that, Corey, we'd have to claim proprietary rights on the last two thousand years! We don't own all the past Christmases, you know."

"Yeah, I guess you're right."

"Listen, stay in touch with me over the holidays, will you? This deal is hanging in the balance, and I want to be able to reach you if I need to."

"I'll keep my ears on," Corey assured him. "Merry Christmas to you and your family."

"Merry Christmas to you, too."

T. J. had no sooner hung up than the intercom buzzed.

"Mr. Robison is on line two," Linda said.

"Did he say what he wants?"

"Just that he wants to talk to you."

"Okay, thanks." T. J. changed lines. "Hi, Bob. What's up?"

Bob Robison was the senior-most producer for Peacock Recording, which produced not only Corey's music, but that of several of T. J.'s other clients as well.

"T. J., I need you to do me a favor. There's a young man in Hopkinsville I want you to hear."

"When?"

"Tonight, if you can."

"Tonight? Oh, I don't know—that's pretty short notice." Wasn't there something going on tonight? He couldn't remember.

"It is, and I apologize for that. It's just that several of my people have recommended him. They say he's another Travis Tritt, and they're after me to sign him. Before I jump into anything, I want an outside opinion."

"Is he represented? I don't want to step on another agent's toes."

"No, he's not. If you like what you hear, you might want to take him on."

"What's his name?"

"Conroy Conrad."

T. J. laughed. "Is that for real, or something he made up?"

"It's the only name I've heard. He's performing a set at the Paradise Lounge at seven. Can you do it?"

T. J. pursed his lips and blew out a breath of air. He checked his calendar but saw nothing. "Bob, wait just a minute." He paged his secretary.

"Yes, sir?"

"Linda, do I have anything scheduled for tonight?"

"Nothing that I'm aware of."

"Okay, thanks." He pushed the button to get back to Bob. "You still there?"

"I'm here."

"All right, I'll do it." He scratched a note on his pad as he spoke. "Paradise Lounge, seven o'clock. Conroy Conrad." He couldn't repress a smile. "I love the name. If he can't sing, it would almost be worth dubbing his voice just so we can use it."

"Thanks, T. J. By the way, how are the negotiations going with our boy Corey?"

"It's looking good. ABC has made an offer, and Heartland is considering topping them."

"Well, here's something you can throw into the mix," Bob said. "We just got the early reports. 'Christmas Past' will be number one on all the major charts tomorrow and, no doubt, through Christmas."

"All right!" T. J. pounded his fist on the desk. "With all the airtime he's been getting, I knew it would go to the top. Thanks for the good news."

For a moment T. J. was both confused and exhilarated, mixing the memories brought on by the strange advertisement for "Christmas Past" with the success and professional achievement of Corey Doolin's newest mega-hit. What was the connection? Or was there any? It was probably just an odd coincidence.

"Yes, well, thank you for bringing him to us."

Linda walked into the office just as he hung up the phone. Middle-aged and rather frumpy looking, she was T. J.'s secret weapon. She had a computerlike mind as far as names and numbers were concerned, and often came to his aid by supplying needed information at just the critical moment in a negotiation.

"Bob just told me that 'Christmas Past' will be number one on the charts tomorrow," T. J. said, smiling broadly.

"Oh, that's wonderful news." Linda set two small boxes on the desk.

"What are those?"

"It's the promotional jewelry you ordered for Corey. I thought you might like to see what it looks like."

T. J. opened the boxes and looked at the two pieces of jewelry. They were identical, except that the brooch was much larger than the lapel pin. Both were gold treble clefs, accented by a single ruby.

"These are pretty nice-looking, aren't they?" he said. "Especially the brooch. And the ruby adds a nice touch, don't you think? It doesn't overstate the obvious, does it?"

"As in 'Ruby Lips'? No, I don't think it overstates at all," Linda said with a grin.

"Wish we could have gotten them sooner. 'Ruby Lips' was number one when we ordered the jewelry."

"Well, it's still on the charts," Linda said. "It's beginning to look as though 'Ruby Lips' might be Corey's signature song. Like Bing's 'White Christmas' and Kenny Rogers' 'Lucille.'"

"If so, it's not a bad one to have."

He examined the brooch carefully. "By the way, what would one of these cost if somebody went out to buy it in a store?"

"That piece would be about fifty dollars, the lapel pin about thirty-five or so."

T. J. looked up in surprise. He usually watched every penny that went out of the office, but he had left this one up to Linda. "Oh, wow, I hope we didn't pay that much."

"No, we got them for less than half that. Besides which, Peacock picked up half the cost."

As Linda turned to leave, T. J. picked up the flyer again. "Linda, do you know where this brochure came from?"

She examined it. "No idea."

"Huh, that's funny. If you didn't put it here, how did it wind up on my desk?"

"I'll see if I can find out."

T. J. studied the advertisement for a moment longer. "No," he finally said. "No need to launch a full-scale investigation. I was just curious."

As Linda left the office, T. J. picked up the phone and called the number listed on the back of the brochure.

"You have reached the line to Christmas Past," an answering-machine voice said. "If you are interested in our service, leave your name, and a place will be reserved for you."

The message was followed by a beep.

"Uh, I don't necessarily want a place reserved, but I would like a little more information. If you could call me back at—"

Before he could give his number, the call was disconnected. T. J. hung up. "You must not want business all that bad," he mumbled to the phone.

Two

"Stand by," the floor director called out, holding up his hand. "Screen is black for down-line commercials."

The studio was large enough to handle five stage sets, four of which were currently dark. The fifth, a set that resembled a well-appointed living room, was brightly lit and, like the lobby and the green room, was decorated for Christmas. In addition to the tree, a few dozen poinsettia plants added a splash of holiday color.

The host of the show, Mrs. T. J. Carmichael, used her maiden name professionally: Madison Bain. Madison had been working television for nearly ten years. Her news-and-talk show pulled a 3.8 rating, two-tenths of a point under Oprah. She had broken important news to the nation; she had interviewed presidents and kings, movie stars, sports figures, and genuine national heroes like firefighters and soldiers.

Many believed that Madison's edgy interview skills lifted her from the mediocrity of other daytime shows, making hers one of the most watched in the country. The management at HeartNet was not unaware that she had received offers from other networks, among them CNN, Fox, and CBS.

Cameras were moved into position, lights were set, and last-minute sound adjustments were made. From force of habit, rather than a genuine need for alteration, Madison touched the soft blonde hair that fell in graceful waves around her face. Her hairdresser and makeup person had already added their finishing touches. A smallish, well-groomed man with thinning hair sat across from her on the set, his suit and tie crisply starched.

"Intro is rolling!" the floor director called.

The monitors in the studio burst into brilliant swirls of color. Then quick cuts of Madison appeared on the screen; Madison laughing, Madison drinking coffee, Madison cooking, and Madison talking to her guests, many of whom were nationally known political and show-business figures.

"And now, from Nashville, Tennessee, this is *Madison Live,* starring Madison Bain!" an exuberant voice-over announced.

"Going live on camera three in five, four, three, two, one!" the floor director said.

Madison waited patiently. By the time the red light came on, she was focused, poised, and smiling brilliantly at camera three.

"We are in the midst of the Christmas season, a season of emotions and memories—especially memories. Perhaps you recall the Christmas pageant in your school, or the Nativity scene on the courthouse lawn. Maybe it was a Christmas celebration in the city park, or Christmas carols filling the air downtown as you hurried about to do your Christmas shopping.

"These are pleasant memories, to be sure, but if my guest today has his way, these will not be memories our children will have when they are grown. Mr. Jack Styles, a lawyer, represents the Myth-Free Coalition, a group that wants to do away with all religion in general, and Christmas in particular."

After cordial greetings, Madison jumped into the first of three segments in the interview. "Mr. Styles, what do you have against Christmas?"

Styles, who had expected to be able to introduce his agenda in his own way, blinked at the opening volley. He took a deep breath. "I believe Christmas represents superstition at its worst, and I don't think people who believe as I do should be forced to celebrate it."

"Do you celebrate Christmas, Mr. Styles?"

"No."

"Have you ever celebrated Christmas?"

"No, I am an atheist."

"Then I don't understand. Since you don't observe Christmas now, and you say you have never observed it, what makes you think you need to take it away from everyone else?"

"I am content to let others celebrate it," Styles said, "so long as they confine it to organized churches and not force their belief system on me."

"But it's okay for you to force your belief system on others?"

"I'm not forcing my belief system on others."

"You believe that there is no God, therefore you want to see nothing that is contrary to that belief. And in order to accomplish that, you want to take Christmas away from everyone else."

"No, I don't. I just don't want the government to sanction religion. And that's what it is doing by putting up a national Christmas tree, or allowing carolers to sing on the courthouse lawn or in the public school gymnasium."

"I have a news clip I'd like you to see," Madison announced, cueing the producer.

The line-feed on the monitor showed Jack Styles standing in front of the New York Museum of American Art. A TV reporter approached him.

Reporter: *Mr. Styles, there is an exhibit in this museum in which a crucifix is being displayed in a soiled toilet bowl. This display has upset many people, and they are calling for its removal, yet you are defending the artist. Why is that?*

Styles: *This nation was founded upon the right of freedom of expression. The purpose of art is to make the viewer think. Just because you do not agree with something is no reason to agitate for its removal.*

Reporter: *If this were a private art showing, I might agree with you. But this is a publicly supported museum. Surely, we should not have to pay for a piece of art that is so offensive to so many.*

Styles: *I say again, it is called freedom of expression. If you don't like that, change the Constitution.*

The line-feed returned to the studio.

"Freedom of expression," Madison said. "Do you still stand by that?"

"Of course."

"Why is it that displaying a religious symbol for the purpose of desecration can be considered freedom of expression, whereas displaying a religious symbol for the purpose of reverence is not?"

"Well it's, uh, much more complicated than that," Styles said.

"Let's uncomplicate it, shall we?" Madison said.

Again, the line-feed on the monitor showed Styles at the New York Museum of American Art.

Styles: *If the people don't want to be offended by this work of art, then my advice to them is: don't look at this particular exhibit.*

When the line-feed returned to the studio, Madison said, "Mr. Styles, I'd like to give you your own advice. If you don't want to be offended by Christmas displays, don't look."

"You are trying to hang on to 'Christmas past,' Ms. Bain," Styles said. "But we have moved beyond that. We no longer need a sense of voodoo to ensure our well-being. And the quicker we disconnect ourselves from these outdated superstitions, the more sane our society will be."

"You call it superstition; some call it faith," Madison replied.

"Superstition, faith—what you will. You have no empirical evidence for the existence of God."

"On the contrary, Mr. Styles. Existence itself is all the empirical evidence we need. On the other hand, as a negative cannot be proven, you have no way to validate your belief that there is no God." Madison paused and turned to the camera. "We'll hear more from Mr. Styles after these messages."

Madison's abrupt cut to commercial left Styles with his mouth hanging open.

"You blindsided me, Ms. Bain," he accused during the commercial break. He qualified his statement, trying to ease the moment. "You have great argumentative skills. You'd make a good attorney."

"It isn't my skill in arguing that makes me a good attorney, Mr. Styles. It is the strength of my case."

"Back in one minute!" the floor director called.

When the show ended Madison picked her way carefully across the cables, around the cameras, and through the myriad of sets as she headed for her dressing room.

"Good show, Madison," a technician said.

"Thanks," she replied, flashing a warm smile at him.

The telephone message light was blinking when she reached her office, and she called her voice mailbox. There she heard a message from T. J.

"Hi, Madison, I caught what I could of the show. You did a great job of putting that guy in his place. Listen, uh, don't wait dinner for me tonight. I'm driving over to Hopkinsville to listen to a singer. I'll be back around midnight."

"No!" Madison said angrily, slamming the phone down. She picked it up again and called T. J.'s cell phone.

"T. J. Carmichael."

"You promised to go to the kids' Christmas pageant," Madison blurted without saying hello.

"Oh," T. J. said sheepishly. "That's what it was. I knew I was supposed to do something tonight—I just couldn't remember what it was."

"Aren't you glad I reminded you? Are we going together, or do you want to meet me there?"

"Didn't you get my message? I'm in Hopkinsville. There's

some guy I need to hear sing. They say he's another Travis Tritt."

"T. J., we don't need another Travis Tritt. We have a Travis Tritt. What we do need is for the two of us to go to our children's Christmas pageant."

"I can't go, Madison. I promised Bob Robison I would listen to this guy."

"And that promise carries more weight than the one you made to your children?"

"You know better than that. This is business."

"Business. Right," Madison said.

"What are they doing having a Christmas pageant in school anyway? I thought those were outlawed. Isn't that what you were just talking about with that lawyer fella?"

"They are outlawed, T. J.," she replied icily. "In public schools. Our children attend Belle Meade Christian Academy, remember?"

"Madison, be reasonable. I'm almost to Hop-town. Even if I turned around now, I wouldn't make it back in time. I'll make it up to them. Explain it to them, and tell them I'm sorry."

"They don't need it explained to them," Madison remarked dryly. "You've disappointed them so often now that they understand quite clearly." She hung the phone up without saying good-bye.

With a sigh of disgust, Madison sat down on the sofa in her dressing room and leaned her head back. Where had their marriage gone offtrack?

Fourteen years ago, Madison was a just-hired reporter for a local Nashville TV station. The station sent her to get an interview with Rebel Casey, an exciting female vocalist who was tearing up the charts. What Madison didn't know was that Rebel was practically a recluse and didn't grant interviews to anyone. The assignment director, who knew that perfectly well, planned to have a big laugh at her expense when she returned to the station, empty-handed and frustrated.

But what the director had not known about was Madison Bain's persistence. She wasn't put off by the first refusal, and while talking to people who might be able to lead her to Rebel, she was introduced to T. J. Carmichael, touted an "up-and-coming artists' rep." Whether moved by Madison's plight or just attracted to her, she never knew, but T. J. came through. And when she returned to the studio with the interview in the can, she not only shocked the features editor, she also assured herself a career in television.

After a brief courtship, Madison and T. J. married. They were very much in love and had two children, Timmy and Christine. In the beginning, even as their careers were taking off, they found time for each other, for their children, and even for God. But now the stress of mutual success gave them very little time for anything else.

Madison was angry with T. J., but when she faced the truth, she knew she was as guilty as he. Just two weeks ago she had stayed late at the studio doing promos while T. J. was deep into negotiations in New York City, leaving their nanny with the sole responsibility of handling a school event.

Madison took off her shoes and put her feet on the coffee table. As she did so, she noticed a colorful holiday flyer. A large, antebellum home, decorated for Christmas, drew her eye.

Picking up the brochure, she examined the photograph on the front for a moment before looking inside. Something about the picture appealed to her—not only the beauty of the house, but the serenity of the scene—perhaps it was because the Christmas decorations were subtle and lacked the commercial flashiness of their own. No gaudy lights outlined the roof, no reindeer and sleigh, no Santa, no elves. There was only the natural greenery of pine and holly, accented with red berries and ribbons.

They seemed to be selling something called Christmas Past. Ironic. Wasn't that what her guest, Jack Styles, had just accused her of . . . trying to hold on to "Christmas Past"?

Her eyes locked on the Scripture from John 3:16, "For God so loved the world, that He gave his only begotten Son, that whosoever believeth in him should not perish but have everlasting life." She knew the verse well and continued reading.

Is your family suffering because life has become too stressful? Has the pressure of life crowded out more important things, such as the love of Christ and your love for one another? We invite you to celebrate a Victorian "Christmas Past" with us. Slip back in time to a gentler era. At Gracehall, Christmas is a celebration of faith, not a frenzy of buying. Here, there are no commercial marathons or legal barriers to Christmas. Join us from December 24 to 26. . . .

"Right," Madison said sarcastically. "We can't get together for an hour-long Christmas pageant. Where are we going to find three whole days?"

When was the last time she and T. J. had been together for three straight days? A sense of sadness and near-desperation gripped her, but she pushed the feelings away. Stuffing the flyer into her purse, Madison put on her shoes, grabbed her coat from the closet, and left for home.

"Have a pleasant evening, Ms. Bain," the security guard said as Madison passed through the monitoring gate.

"Thank you, George." Punching the green button, she pushed the door open and stepped outside.

"Ladies and gentlemen, Madison has left the building," she announced quietly to no one in particular.

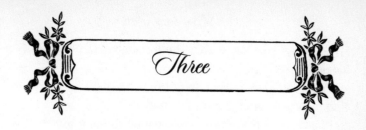

Three

The waitress wore a low-cut green blouse and a very short green skirt. Her shapely legs were encased in dark hose, but the effect was ruined by the run in the back of her left leg. Although she didn't look a day over nineteen, her pretty face was drawn from exhaustion.

"You want something to drink?" she asked T. J., as she extended her bottom lip to blow away the errant tendril of red hair that had fallen across her forehead.

"Coffee."

"Coffee? That's all?"

"I have to drive back to Nashville tonight," he said. It was easier than saying he didn't drink, which always got one of two reactions: either hostility from those who felt accused because they did drink, or a quiet, understanding nod from those who believed him to be a recovered alcoholic. The truth was, he just didn't like it that much, and the few times he had tried it in his youth, booze had made him sick.

"Cream and sugar?"

"Lots of cream," T. J. said. "And leave room in the cup for me to add it."

"All right."

"Oh, and uh . . . this is so you won't get gypped out of your tip because I'm not drinking." He handed the girl a ten-dollar bill.

"Thanks!" she said with a genuine smile. "I'll get your coffee right away."

As the waitress walked away from the table, T. J. saw the club manager walking onto the stage.

"Ladies and gentlemen, the Paradise Lounge is proud to present the musical stylings of Conroy Conrad!" The manager stepped down, and a young man wearing black pants and a black shirt, trimmed in silver, stepped up to the microphone. Without a word of introduction, he began playing and singing "Ruby Lips."

"Mom," eight-year-old Timmy said as he went up to bed that night. "Why didn't Dad come to our pageant?"

"Oh, you know how it is, honey," Madison said matter-of-factly. "Something came up at his job."

"Are you mad at him because he didn't come?"

"No, I'm not angry. I'm . . . disappointed."

"You looked mad when you came to school. It seems like you and Dad have been mad at each other a lot lately."

"We both work very hard, Timmy, and sometimes our work makes us a little short-tempered. But not really mad. Now you go to sleep."

Madison smiled down at her son as he climbed into his bed, and she bent to pull up his covers. Timmy could see that her eyes were glistening with tears.

"You and Christine were wonderful in the pageant tonight. I was very proud of you both." As she leaned over the bed to kiss Timmy good night, she added, "Don't forget to say your prayers."

"I won't."

Timmy watched his mother leave the room, and as she shut the door he closed his eyes to pray.

"Dear Lord, this is me . . . Timmy Carmichael. I know lots of kids are probably praying to you right now about things they want for Christmas. You remember that last night I told You all I want for Christmas is for Mom and Dad to stop being mad at each other? Well, that's still what I want. I know they love each other, but the way things are going, I'm afraid they might stop loving each other. Please find some way to help them. In Jesus' name. Amen."

As T. J. drove back to Nashville that night, he cracked the window in the car just enough to let the air circulate. The outside air was cold, but he wanted to carry away the tobacco odor that clung to his clothes. It may have been his imagination, but it seemed to him that everyone in the Paradise Lounge was smoking and he had watched the show through a fog bank.

Conroy Conrad had been pretty good, even though he sang only cover songs, including two more that Corey Doolin had made popular. Singing only cover songs wasn't an insurmountable problem, because original music wasn't that difficult to come by. But when T. J. talked to him after the set, he found that the young man was a little too full of himself. While confidence was certainly necessary for success,

T. J. firmly believed that singers should never cross the line into arrogance unless they had the talent to support it. In his opinion, Conroy Conrad did not.

He would give Bob Robison as accurate a report as he could, but T. J. had no interest in representing the kid. He'd wasted an evening and had nothing to show for it but an angry wife.

As T. J. thought about Madison, he realized that he found her no less attractive now than he had in the beginning. If anything, she was even more beautiful, and he respected her work. He laughed somewhat bitterly. She had more than held her own with the atheist who had been her guest today.

He wasn't sure exactly when things started going sour in their marriage. Remembering her cool response on the phone earlier brought back memories of recent arguments between them, a sense of the growing distance and even alienation that he felt. Did she feel the same way? Did she even think about him when he wasn't around? When he wasn't around . . .

In T. J.'s business, he was often surrounded by beautiful women. And with that sixth sense that some women have, many of them perceived that things weren't going that well in his marriage. Several of them had offered T. J. the opportunity to stray, some by sending very subtle signals, others with out-and-out invitations. But despite many opportunities, not once during his entire marriage had he been unfaithful to his wife.

Somehow, though, fidelity and a healthy appreciation of all her good qualities didn't seem to be enough. He was failing her in more important ways, and he knew it. In retrospect, he should have passed on listening to Conroy Conrad tonight and gone to the children's pageant. But after years of following his career wherever it took him, T. J. found it difficult to change course.

It was 11:45 P.M. when he opened the front door to their house. He tried to come in quietly so he wouldn't wake anyone, but to his surprise he found Madison waiting up for him.

"Madison? What are you doing still awake?"

"Waiting for you," she answered.

"Waiting for me? Why? Is everything all right?"

"No," she replied. "Everything is not all right."

"Did something happen to one of the kids?"

"It's not the kids, T. J. It's us."

"Us." He hung his coat in the closet.

Looking over at the table beside her, T. J. saw a small pile of soiled tissues. "Madison, I know that things aren't going as well as they should in our marriage—"

"Marriage?" Madison asked. "What marriage? We aren't married, T. J. Not really. We're roommates."

"Well, if we are, we're friendly roommates, aren't we?" He smiled, trying to ease the pain of the moment.

"This has gone too far for jokes. Marriage is supposed to be a partnership. Parenting is a partnership. When was the last time we did something as a family? It's always me taking the kids somewhere, or you taking them somewhere, or sometimes the nanny filling in for both of us. We never do things together."

"We both have high-pressure jobs," T. J. said. "And let's face it, we are both very successful." He leaned back into the lounge chair cushions.

"Yes, but at what price? I can't even remember the last time we sat down as a family for a meal that wasn't take-out."

"It's not all that bad, is it? I mean, we never fight, or say hateful things to each other."

"Sometimes I wish we would fight. At least that way I would know that there was some . . . some passion in our marriage. There's nothing there anymore."

"Where is this going?" T. J. asked.

"Where do all marriages go when there is nothing left?"

"Are you saying you want a divorce?"

Madison took a deep breath. "No, I don't want a divorce. I don't think anybody ever really *wants* a divorce. But the way things are between us, I think it's inevitable. And that being the case, I think we should do it as quickly and painlessly as possible."

T. J. snorted. "Do you know some way to have a divorce without pain?"

"No, I don't," she admitted in a quiet, choked voice.

"Divorce is going to be awfully hard on the kids, don't you think?"

"It will be a lot easier on them if we do it now, while they are young enough to recover. And while there is still goodwill between us." Madison brushed a tear from her eye.

"If there is 'goodwill' between us, then why are we talking about divorce?"

"T. J., are you going to sit there and tell me that you haven't considered this possibility?"

"No, I can't tell you that." He took a swallow of coffee. "I have thought about it . . . feared it." He shook his head, wondering if this conversation could really be happening.

"If we are going to do it, let's do it now, while we still have enough feelings for each other not to want to cause each other any more pain. We can work out an equitable way of sharing the children. And since we are both economically successful, I don't think there will be any financial demands."

"You know, there is a way we could make this work," T. J. said.

"How?" Madison demanded, her skepticism showing in her voice and face.

"If one of us would give up our career."

"'One of us.' You mean if *I* would give up *my* career, don't you?"

"I know you don't want to hear it, Madison, but that would be the more logical choice. I earn more than you do, and besides that, I have two-dozen musicians who depend upon me for their own livings."

"Do you really think that would work, T. J.? Don't you think I might get bitter and start blaming you?"

"I don't know," T. J. sighed. "Maybe you're right. Maybe it is too late for us. But what about the kids? How will we tell them? And when?"

"I'm not sure how to tell them." Madison felt numbed by the way the conversation had gone, but she tried to speak matter-of-factly. "But I have a very strong opinion as to when."

"When, then?"

"I want to wait until after Christmas. Something like this could ruin Christmas for them forever."

"I have an idea. That is, if you're up to it. Why don't we go somewhere for Christmas? All of us, as a family. It might be our last . . ." T. J. let out a long breath. "Our last Christmas as a family."

"Where would we go?"

"Well, Corey is going to the Bahamas. We could go there."

"Absolutely not," Madison said. "If you get down there with Corey, just how much time do you think you would spend with the kids?"

"You're right. What about taking an ocean cruise?"

Madison vetoed that one too. "No way. The last thing I want to do is be trapped on board a ship with a thousand people who are trying to give me ideas for my TV show."

"How about Europe? You won't be as recognizable in Europe."

"That would be all right, I guess. Though the hassle of flying overseas now doesn't really appeal to me."

"All right, then you come up with an idea," T. J. challenged. "Where would you like to go?"

"I don't really know," Madison admitted. "Somewhere quiet, a little out of the way. A place where both of us could spend some quality time with the kids, and maybe even get in touch with Christmas itself."

"What does that mean, 'get in touch with Christmas?'"

"I'm not exactly sure. Maybe it's because of the show I did today, but I just realized that we don't really celebrate Christmas. I don't know that we ever have—not the true Christmas. I know I'm not making sense, but . . . I want to go to a *feeling* as much as to a place."

"Well, I don't know how to—" He stopped midsentence.

"Wait a minute . . . maybe I do know how! How would you like to go to Possum Hollow? Or, as I'm sure the folks say there, Possum Holler."

"What are you talking about?"

"I saw something today. It was an ad for 'Christmas Past.' I left it in the office, but I can get it in the morning."

"Christmas Past? There's no need to wait until morning." Madison picked up her purse.

"What do you mean?"

She opened her purse and removed a brochure. "Is this what you're talking about?"

"Yeah, that's the one. Where'd you get that?"

"It was in my dressing room after the show." She looked at the back of the brochure. "You're right, it is Possum Hollow," she said. "I wonder where that is."

"In the Smokies somewhere. Anyway, how would you like to go there? I gather it's some sort of historical Christmas thing. It would be . . ."

"Serene?" Madison asked.

"Yes. I could do with a little serenity. I think we all could."

"Don't you think going to a place like that might be a little awkward for us? I mean, pretending to be happily married?"

"All right, let's pretend not to be married. Let's just pretend to be happy roommates, sharing a Christmas vacation with a couple of swell kids," T. J. suggested.

"I don't know if I can do that," Madison said.

"Madison, we owe the kids this. And I think it would make it easier to tell them afterward."

"All right. I guess we can try."

"Good." T. J. turned the brochure over so he could see the information on the back, then picked up the phone.

"What are you doing?"

"Making a reservation."

"No one will be there at this time of night."

"It's an electronic reservation. You just leave your name with the answering machine."

"How do you know?"

"Because I called them earlier today." T. J. reached for the phone.

Madison looked puzzled. "You mean you were already thinking about going?"

"Not really, but the name intrigued me. Didn't you notice? It's the same as the title of Corey's newest song."

"I guess I didn't make the connection."

"Well, believe me, I did. I just wanted to find out who these people are and what this is all about . . . but all I got was a machine."

"Wait a minute. You know nothing about them, but you are still willing to go?"

"How bad can it be? If we don't like it, we can always get in the car and drive away."

"I suppose you're right. Okay, give them a call."

He picked up the phone and punched in the number. "Yes," he said, when the machine answered. "I'd like reservations for Mr. and Mrs. T. J. Carmichael and two children, a boy age eight, and a girl age six. We'll be there from December 24 until the 26th." He hung up.

"That's it? That's all we have to do? You didn't even give them a credit card number."

"I don't want to leave a credit card number on an answering machine. They can take it when we check in. And speaking of checking in, let's go to bed, shall we? I'm dead tired."

"All right," Madison agreed.

They walked down the hallway together, but when they reached the bedroom door, Madison didn't stop.

"Where are you going?"

"Under the circumstances, I think one of us should sleep in the guest room until this is over."

"You aren't planning on having separate rooms when we check in to this Christmas Past, are you?"

"No."

"Then why now?"

"I just . . . I just think we should."

He stared at her for a long moment, then let out a resigned sigh. "All right, Madison. If this is what you want, I won't fight you over it."

"Thank you. This is what I want."

"Good night," T. J. said.

Madison paused for a second before opening the door to the guest room. "Good night," she replied, then stepped into the room and closed the door behind her.

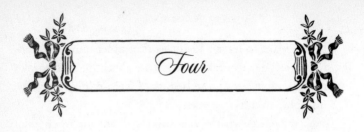

Four

December 24

Traveling on I-40 about 120 miles east of Nashville, the Mercedes S-Class Sedan cruised at eighty miles per hour, the ride so smooth that the passengers were barely aware of movement. Despite the holiday, T. J. had one hand on the steering wheel, the other on the telephone that was pressed to his ear. Madison had her seat tilted back and felt enveloped in the soft leather, looking through the window at the morning sun drifting through the trees of the Smoky Mountains. She did her best not to dwell on the tense conversations of the last few days, which had left her feeling farther and farther away from her husband.

Timmy and Christine sat in the backseat, Timmy playing with a Gameboy while Christine held her favorite stuffed bear. They rarely fought outright, though they were as competitive and feisty as their parents.

T. J. gripped the telephone. "Yes," he said. "'Christmas Past' has been on the charts since the day it was released, never lower than number four."

He was quiet for the response on the other end.

"Yes, I expect it will fall off the charts after the Christmas holidays, but it'll be back on next year. I mean, look at 'White Christmas.'"

Another response that Madison and the kids could not hear.

"Yes, I am comparing it to 'White Christmas.' It has that same classic quality."

Another silence. "Yes, Madison is right here beside me. I'll tell her. And remember, you can reach me on my cell for the next few days. You'll let me know if anything breaks?"

T. J. turned the phone off, then hung it from the little hook attached to the console. "Evan says hi."

"I thought we were supposed to have a few days of—what was it you called it—serenity?" Madison folded her arms across her chest.

"We are."

"But you plan to keep your cell on for the whole time, right?"

"Come on, Madison. I have to stay in touch with Evan, you know that. Right now Corey's TV special is just hanging there. It could go either way."

"You don't have to explain it to me," she said. "It's none of my business anymore."

"Mama, what do you mean, it's none of your business anymore?" Timmy asked from the backseat. Behind his brown eyes and easy smile was a quick study of character and wisdom beyond his years.

T. J. and Madison glanced at each other.

"Uh, she just means I'm the agent, she's the star," T. J. said.

"Mama is the star, isn't she?" Christine asked.

"Yes, she is," T. J. agreed.

"Tell me about where we're going," Timmy interjected. "Is it like Disney World?"

"I suppose you could say it's a little like Disney World," Madison said.

"You mean they'll have rides and stuff?" Christine asked.

"Well, no, not exactly."

"They'll probably have carriages, wagons, that sort of thing," T. J. suggested.

"Yes, I'm sure they'll have those," Madison agreed.

"And horses?" Christine asked.

"I'm sure they'll have horses," her mother assured her.

"I like horses."

"But I still don't know what it is," Timmy said.

"Do you remember this summer when we went to the Civil War battle?" T. J. asked.

"Yes," Timmy replied excitedly.

"And do you remember how old everything seemed? The guns, the uniforms, even the clothes the people in the camp were wearing?"

"But it wasn't really old, Dad. They just pretended they were back in the olden days."

"Yes, that's true. They were what are called reenactors. That's sort of what this will be like."

"Are they going to shoot guns again?" Christine asked. "I didn't like that. It hurt my ears."

"No, there won't be any guns," Madison said. "It's a re-enactment, only this time, instead of war, it will be Christmas."

"But Christmas is Christmas, isn't it? How can you act it?" Timmy asked.

"That's a good question, Timmy. This will be . . . Christmas as it used to be," Madison said.

"Like when you and Daddy were little?"

Madison laughed with genuine pleasure at her daughter's words. "Hardly. It's more like it was when my great-*grandparents* were little."

"Wow! That's a long, long, *long* time ago," Timmy said.

"Do you mind if I turn on the radio?" asked T. J., fiddling with the buttons on the dashboard. He found a satellite station, and instantly the car was filled with music.

Madison settled back in her seat, using the music as a means of weaving a little cocoon around herself. As I-40 curved like a black ribbon around the side of the mountain, she looked over the steel railing and down into the valley below. She could see a little town with no more than two- or three-dozen houses, dominated by a single white church with a towering steeple.

For a moment, though she didn't voice her thoughts aloud, Madison wished that they lived down there in that picturesque little village. How nice it would be if T. J. were a farmer, or ran a feed store or a filling station. She imagined herself as a schoolteacher, or perhaps a store clerk. She saw children walking home from school, not only because the school would be close, but because it would be safe for them to do so.

If they lived there, their only contact with the outside world would be the traffic on I-40, and as the interstate was high up along the mountainside, those cars would be as remote as airliners passing overhead. The family would be in a self-contained, uncontaminated world, free of the stresses and pressures of their high-profile occupations.

She had no idea what denomination the church was, but

she didn't care. How wonderful it must be for the people who attended that church. She was sure that they knew each other, and knew and were known by the pastor. They greeted each other by name after the Sunday service, and perhaps invited friends home for a dinner of fried chicken.

How long had it been since they had been to church as a family? For that matter, how long had it been since she had been to church at all?

She had made such a convincing defense of her Christian beliefs when the atheist lawyer had been her guest on the show that she'd received hundreds of letters and e-mails from believers, thanking her. But in retrospect her well-delivered debating points made her feel like a hypocrite. She had passed herself off as a good Christian, when in fact she had not been active in church for years.

"T. J., let's get off the interstate," Madison suggested.

"What? Why? We're making great time."

"No reason. I'd just like to take one of the smaller, back roads is all."

"All right," he said agreeably. "With GPS, it's not like we're going to get lost or anything."

He turned north on the next exit, and within a few minutes it was as if the interstate didn't even exist. They traveled along a narrow blacktop road, winding through the mountains and alongside swiftly moving streams and forested glades. For half an hour no one spoke. Even the kids seemed lost in their own thoughts or in the music on the radio.

T. J. broke the reverie. "Well, it's a narrow road, but at least there's not much traffic."

"Much traffic? How about *no* traffic? I haven't seen a car since we left the interstate," Madison said.

"Yeah, now that you mention it. This would be a bad place to have a wreck, wouldn't it? No telling when someone would find you."

"T. J., don't even joke about such a thing," Madison said.

"Oh, listen. It's 'Christmas Past.'"

Corey Doolin's voice, deep and melodic, filled the car.

> In a flophouse in Toledo
> Across from the depot
> A candle burned into the night
>
> I saw him sittin' there
> On an old broken chair
> His eyes were shining in the light
>
> He started in humming
> His fingers were strumming
> Though no guitar was there
>
> I wandered over near him
> In order to hear him
> And this is what I did hear.
>
> Do you remember that Christmas of old
> When the love of the Christ child was worth more than gold?
> When Jesus was the reason, to celebrate the season
> Do you remember that Christmas of old?

"What do you think about that song?" T. J. asked when it was over.

"I think he sings it beautifully," Madison said.

"I do too," Christine added.

"Why, thank you, darlin,'" T. J. said with some pride of ownership.

The radio had started another number, but right in the middle of the song, it stopped.

"What happened?" T. J. glanced at the dashboard.

"We must have lost the station," Madison suggested.

"We can't lose the station, it's satellite radio," T. J. insisted.

"Sometimes satellite signals can be temporarily blocked," Madison said. "That's why we have such an array of dishes at HeartNet."

The GPS screen went dark.

"You're right, we must've lost the satellite," T. J. said. "GPS just went down too. Okay, let's see what we can get over the air."

He touched the scan button, and the numbers flashed by on the dial until they reached the end, then they began recycling.

"That's funny," he said. "Nothing on the dial . . ."

"Well, if we can't access the satellite, then we probably can't get a regular station either."

"We ought to get something. Not clear, maybe, but something. I mean, we're not even picking up static."

"Must be the radio."

"Oh great," T. J. said in disgust. "Now the blacktop has ended."

The road turned to gravel, then to dirt, and T. J. had to slow to about thirty miles per hour.

"This can't be right," Madison said after a few minutes. "We must have taken a wrong turn somewhere."

"A turn? What turn? There hasn't even been a place *to* turn since we left the interstate."

"T. J., do you have any idea where we are?" Madison asked.

"No, not really," T. J. answered. "I didn't see any signs on the road when we left I-40, but I wasn't paying that much attention. Did you see any signs?"

"No, I didn't. Why don't we see if we can find our place on the map?"

T. J. shook his head. "There's no map in the car. Who needs a map when you've got global positioning system?"

"Yes. But we don't have GPS, do we?"

"No. We don't."

"We shouldn't have left the interstate."

"You're the one who wanted to take a side road."

"I know. But now I think we should go back to I-40."

"Come on, Madison. You're talking about backtracking at least forty miles. I'd like to get there before nightfall."

"Get where? We don't even know where we are."

"This road is bound to come out somewhere."

"I don't feel good about this, T. J.," Madison said. "Being on a narrow, dirt road way back in the mountains? It's a little disconcerting."

"All right, all right. If it will make you feel better, I'll turn around as soon as I can find a place."

"Thank you. It will make me feel better."

"Dad, did we bring any batteries?" Timmy asked.

"Batteries? For what?"

"For my Gameboy. It just quit."

"Well, I could handle the radio and the GPS going out, but your Gameboy? Now we really are in a fix."

"Sarcasm does not become you, Dad."

T. J. laughed. "You learned that little comment from your mother, didn't you?"

"Yes," Timmy said, laughing as well.

Suddenly the engine quit, and the car coasted to a stop.

"What happened?" Madison asked.

"The engine just died." He turned the key but got no response.

"T. J., don't play games," Madison said. "I told you this is giving me the willies."

"I'm not playing games, Madison. In case you didn't notice, the car stopped, and I can't get it started. We're stranded."

"You should have checked the car before we left."

"What do you mean, I should've checked the car? This is a Mercedes with less than twenty thousand miles, for crying out loud. It was serviced two weeks ago. Just what is there to check besides fuel?"

Madison pulled her cell phone from her purse. "I'm going to call AAA," she said. "I just hope I can figure out how to tell them where we are."

"The last mile marker I saw before we left the interstate was 338. Maybe if you tell them that, and describe the area to them, they can figure out where we are."

Madison opened her phone, then groaned. "Oh, no," she said. "The battery is dead."

"How can that be? I charged both phones all night long," T. J. said. "You must have a short in yours." He picked up his own phone. "What's the number for AAA?"

"It's—"

"Never mind. I'm not getting a signal anyway."

"T. J., this . . . this is bad, isn't it?" Madison asked.

"It's not very good," he admitted.

"Mama, I'm scared," Christine said, sensing her mother's anxiety.

"Don't be afraid, darling, everything's going to be all right," Madison replied, though she didn't sound very convincing even to herself.

"Wouldn't it be way cool if we had to stay here all night?" Timmy suggested.

"Mama, I don't want to sleep here," Christine said.

"Oh, I doubt we'll have to stay here all night," T. J. replied. "Someone is sure to come along before then."

"I hope so, but who? We left the interstate over an hour ago, and we haven't seen one other car since that time."

"Yes, but we are on a road, which means that someone will be along eventually. We'll just wait."

"If this is a logging road or something, there may not be anyone on it until spring."

T. J. shrugged. "It won't be that long."

"I hope you're right."

"I hope so too," he said.

Five

"Dad, what's that noise?" Timmy pressed his nose against the window.

"What noise?"

"That *tick-tick-tick* sound coming from the front of the car."

"That's just the engine," T. J. said with as much confidence as he could muster. "It makes that sound when the engine is cooling."

After a moment or two the engine quit ticking, and then there was only the sound of a nearby stream as it broke over water-polished rocks. The babble of the brook was augmented by the distant trill of a bird.

Several does slipped out of the nearby trees, looked around cautiously, then moved down to the stream.

"Children, look at the deer," Madison said quietly.

"Oh, neat!" Christine exclaimed. She, too, was watching the world outside the car's windows as if it were a TV show.

"What are we going to do for lunch?" Madison asked.

"We've got a while until lunchtime," T. J. said. "Let's not worry about it until then."

They all grew quiet again. Madison and T. J. looked at each other, and each said a silent prayer.

"This is not good," T. J. said after a while, his frustration evident. "I need to be in touch. If Evan is trying to get hold of me now, and can't, it could mess everything up."

"We're sitting out here in the middle of nowhere, no food, no water, and, I might add, no way to keep warm if we have to spend the night—and you're worried about business." Madison stared at him, shaking her head.

"I can't stop the world, Madison. Besides, the ball is in Evan's court. There's nothing I can do now but wait for HeartNet to make a decision."

"T. J., you didn't put me into the bargaining mix, did you?"

"Put you into the bargaining mix? What are you talking about? How would I do that?"

"By telling HeartNet you would guarantee that I would stay with them if they would do this."

"Are you thinking about leaving HeartNet?" T. J. couldn't contain his surprise. He knew that communication between them had dwindled, but he couldn't believe she wouldn't tell him something this important.

"I have received some tempting offers. You know that."

"Yes, I know. But are you thinking of accepting one of them?"

"No, but—"

"Don't worry, you have nothing to do with this deal," T. J. said flatly.

"You're sure you haven't even intimated something like that?"

T. J. couldn't keep his voice from rising a pitch. "This may come as a surprise to you, Madison Bain, but even before you became a TV star, I was negotiating deals."

"I'm sorry, I didn't mean— It's just, well, it would make my position with the network very delicate."

"I know it would," he said. "That's why I would never do anything like that."

They had been waiting for almost forty-five minutes, and although the car was still warm, T. J. knew that if they had to stay here all day, it would get cold after the sun went down. He was just beginning to think about that possibility when Timmy spoke.

"Dad, somebody's coming."

"What? Where?"

"Up there." Timmy pointed through the windshield.

"I don't see anyone."

"There! There it is," Timmy said.

About a quarter of a mile up the road, just where it curved out of sight, T. J. saw something as well. "Yes, I see it now," he said with a big smile. His smile faded, however, when he saw that the vehicle approaching them was a horse-drawn carriage. "What in the world . . . ?"

T. J. looked over toward Madison. "Amish, do you think?"

"I don't know," she replied with a shrug.

The family watched the carriage as it drew close enough for them to see the man and woman sitting in the front seat.

"No, I don't think so," Madison said. "Look at her dress."

"It looks old-fashioned to me. So does his suit."

"Yes, but the dress is bright lavender, and he's not wearing a beard. Besides, that doesn't look like any Amish carriage I've seen before."

"You're right. Well, whoever—or whatever—they are, at this point beggars can't be choosers. I'm going to stop them. If they'll stop."

T. J. got out of the car and started up the road toward the approaching carriage. Smiling, he held up his hand.

The driver pulled back on the reins, then set the brake. "Hello," he said.

"Hi," T. J. replied. "Am I glad to see you."

"Are you in distress?" the driver asked.

T. J. pointed to his car. "Yes, I'm broken down, and I can't call AAA because I can't get a signal on my cell," he said. "I was wondering if you could help."

"I will be glad to do what I can. But I'm afraid your conveyance may be too heavy for my horses to pull."

"Oh, I wouldn't expect you to pull us anywhere. But perhaps you could give us a lift to someplace where we can call for help."

"A lift?"

"A ride," T. J. said.

The man smiled mysteriously. "A ride, yes, of course I will. My wife and I are going to a Christmas celebration. We would be happy to have you join us."

"Oh, I wouldn't want to impose on your Christmas celebration, but, as you can see, we are in a bit of a fix here." He turned and motioned for the others to come. Madison, Timmy, and Christine swiftly exited the car, slamming the doors behind them.

"What sort of conveyance do you call that?" the carriage driver said.

"It's a Mercedes. You'd think it would be more dependable."

"Mercedes?" The driver seemed baffled. "Well, I have no name for my carriage, but the horses are Rhoda and Harry. And, noble steeds that they are, they have never let me down."

"Your horses' names are Rhoda and Harry?" Christine asked.

"Yes indeed. And who would you be?" the driver of the carriage asked.

"I'm Christine."

"Oh, forgive me," T. J. said. "I haven't introduced myself, or my family. My daughter, Christine, you just met. That's my son, Timmy, and this is my wife, Madison. I'm T. J. Carmichael."

"It is good to meet you, Mr. Carmichael. I'm Angus MacLeod, and this is my wife, Cora."

"Why are you dressed like that?" Timmy asked.

"Timmy!" Madison blurted.

Angus laughed. "Don't scold the lad, Mrs. Carmichael. I expect it is rather strange to see us in Sunday clothes on a working day. We're dressed like this because we're going to celebrate Christmas at Gracehall."

"Gracehall?" T. J. said with a mixture of surprise and relief. "Wait a minute. You're going to Gracehall?"

"Yes."

T. J. smiled broadly. "Oh, well, that explains the clothes and the carriage then, doesn't it? We are scheduled to celebrate Christmas at Gracehall as well."

"Quite a happy coincidence, I would say," MacLeod said. "Isn't it a good thing we came along?"

"I had no idea we were so close. How far is it?"

MacLeod pulled a watch from his pocket, opened the cover, and examined it. "We'll be there in time for lunch."

"Did you hear that? You don't need to worry about lunch. We'll be there in time."

"Are we going to ride in the wagon?" Christine asked.

"Yes," T. J. said. "But it's not a wagon; it's a carriage. And, I'll say this for you, Mr. MacLeod, you are certainly going all-out for this Christmas Past thing. I'm very impressed with your carriage."

"Thank you, I'm very proud of it. It was not in such good condition when I purchased it, but my father-in-law helped me restore it. Like our Lord, he is a carpenter, and very good."

"You'll get no argument from me." T. J. ran his hands along the dashboard of the carriage. "You and your father-in-law did a remarkably good job. It's about the most authentic-looking carriage I have ever seen."

"Have you any luggage?"

"Yes, just a minute and I'll get it."

"I'll help you retrieve it."

"Thank you, but my son can help. Come on, Timmy."

"Okay, Dad."

T. J. pointed his key ring toward the car and clicked it to open the trunk. Nothing happened. "That's dumb of me. If everything else is down, then the remote won't work either." He used the key to open the trunk and then, after taking out the luggage, found that the only way he could secure the car was to lock every door manually.

"That's it," he said as he and Timmy put the two large and

two small suitcases into the rear of the carriage. "As soon as we get back to Nashville, I'm trading that car."

"You just bought it. I thought you were so proud of it," Madison said.

"Well, I was until all this happened. It's turned into a worthless . . . expensive, but worthless . . . pile of junk."

With the luggage secure, T. J., Madison, Timmy, and Christine climbed into the backseat.

"Are you ready?" MacLeod asked.

"All set," T. J. answered.

MacLeod slapped the reins against his team. "Giddyup, there!" The horses lurched forward. The carriage was well-sprung and rode much more comfortably than T. J. had expected.

MacLeod's carriage had approached them from the front, which meant that once they got under way they were retracing the same route they had just covered in the car. They were on the road for about forty minutes, when Madison made an observation.

"Strange that we aren't back up on the blacktop yet," she said. "We didn't make a turn anywhere, did we?"

"No, I don't think so. It's just that we are going a lot slower now than when we were in the car. And we drove at least fifteen miles after we left the blacktop. We certainly haven't came back that far since Mr. MacLeod picked us up."

"I guess you're right."

They passed a small farm consisting of a house and a few outbuildings, including a barn. A man in the backyard was pumping water, and as they drove by, Angus waved and called out to him.

"Hello, Thomas! Will you and your family be coming to Gracehall for the Christmas party?"

"Wouldn't miss it for the world. We'll be there before lunch," Thomas called back.

Two children, a boy about twelve and a girl who looked to be about Timmy's age, came out of the house to wave at the carriage. Timmy and Christine waved back.

"Look, Dad, they're dressed up too," Timmy said. "We should have dressed up."

"The brochure said nothing about coming in period costume," T. J. replied.

"I know, but we should have thought about it," Madison said. "It would have been more fun."

T. J. leaned forward to speak to MacLeod. "That man, Thomas, is he a friend of yours?"

"Yes, Thomas Duncan by name. Those children you saw were his grandchildren, come to spend Christmas with Thomas and his wife."

"It's nice that they can have their grandchildren visit them," Madison said.

"There are no finer people in the whole state, if you ask me. Thomas is from the other side of Possum Hollow, but he went away to fight in the war when he was a young man, and come here to settle when he got back."

"Were you in the war?"

"I was not, sir. I'll be honest with you, Mr. Carmichael, I couldn't see that fighting that war was the right thing to do. A lot of folks hereabout didn't take too kindly to me for me taking a stand against it, but I had to do what I thought was right. It's been more'n thirty years now, and things have settled back down. But that was back in the sixties, and enough time has passed so that those who went, like Thomas, and those who stayed behind, like me, can be friends again."

T. J. said, "Well, the sixties were pretty tumultuous, but I think now that as we look back on that period, people on both sides of the question are willing to respect a stand on conscience. Of course, that's just my observation. I was too young either to go away and fight, or to stay behind and join the antiwar demonstrations. And to be honest with you, I don't know which side I would have come down on. I'm just glad I didn't have to make a decision."

"Yes, sir. Well, I just pray to the Lord that such a thing never divides our nation again," Angus said.

"Amen to that."

Several minutes later they passed another house.

"Well, you see?" T. J. said. "We weren't in as much trouble as we thought. There are farms and houses all over the place. Even if Mr. MacLeod hadn't come along, it wouldn't have taken us very long to walk to one of these places."

"Yes, I see. It just seems strange to me that we didn't see any of them when we drove by," Madison commented.

"We just weren't looking for them, that's all. As you recall, we were a little discombobulated about being on a dirt road."

After a few more minutes they turned off the road and started up an even smaller one, little more than a lane. A wooden sign alongside read "County Road 4."

"Wait a minute. *This* is County Road 4?" T. J. asked.

"Yes, this is the road for Gracehall."

T. J. turned and spoke to Madison. "I could've sworn we didn't pass any turnoffs. Evidently we drove right past it."

"Even if we had seen it, I doubt we would have known what it was," Madison said. "This looks more like a driveway than a public throughway. I mean, you could barely get a car through here."

"Yeah, well, county roads and farm-to-market roads are sometimes pretty primitive," T. J. said. "But what bothers me is the fact that this is the address for Gracehall. A bed-and-breakfast on this kind of road? To tell you the truth, I'm beginning to wonder if we might not have made a mistake in coming. This could turn out to be a little more quaint than we counted on."

"Let's not pass judgment yet. After all, that was a pretty slick brochure. I don't think anyone could put out something like that unless they were legitimate," Madison said. "And besides, right now, what choice do we have?"

"I suppose you're right."

"Oh, look, there it is!" Madison pointed to a big white house at the end of the road. "Oh, T. J., it's beautiful! It looks exactly like the picture on the cover."

"Yes, it does, doesn't it?"

"Look at the waterwheel. Talk about quaint!"

The waterwheel was attached to the side of a small, unpainted structure, and it operated by an artificial waterfall, caused by damming the stream to form a large pond. The wheel turned slowly.

"It appears to be working," T. J. said.

"Yes, it is working," said Angus from the front seat.

"That's where the judge grinds his corn into meal and his wheat into flour."

"You mean he actually makes his own cornmeal and flour?" Madison asked, amazed.

"Not only his, but he is very generous with his neighbors," Angus said. "The judge says that God put the stream there for everyone."

"That's very nice of him."

"The judge truly is quality folk."

Angus MacLeod pulled the team and carriage into a large curved driveway in front of the house. T. J. counted at least five more carriages parked there.

"Boy, the other folks are really going all-out for this re-enactment thing, aren't they? Who would've thought there would be this many carriages?"

"I imagine a lot of them are local," Madison said. "This is probably something they do every year, and the carriages and costumes just add to the overall atmosphere."

A dignified-looking man in a nineteenth-century blue frock coat and mustard-colored pants came out to meet the carriage. An attractive and much younger woman, also in nineteenth-century dress, stood by his side.

"Oh, here comes our host, Judge Ragsdale, and his wife," MacLeod said.

"That's his wife?" T. J. exclaimed before he could stop himself.

"She's his second wife. His first wife died of the cholera some years back," Angus explained.

"Cholera? In this day and age?"

"Even the best medicine sometimes cannot prevent—that is, when God calls . . . "

"I see." But he didn't. Looking at Madison, T. J. betrayed his confusion. Was this part of the "fiction" of Gracehall or the reality of life in the country?

"She's been very good for him. She gave him what his first wife could not—a child."

T. J. climbed down from the carriage, then turned to help Madison. Christine held up her arms and he lifted her down, but Timmy jumped.

"Good morning," their host said, smiling broadly and extending his hand. "I'm Judge John Ragsdale, and this is my wife, Sylvia. Welcome to Gracehall."

"Thank you," T. J. said as he shook hands. "Uh, look, I apologize for our clothes. We didn't know it would be in period costume."

"Nonsense, your clothes are fine. I'm just glad you made it here."

"Under the circumstances, we are too. Our car broke down, and if Mr. MacLeod hadn't come along when he did, we would still be stranded. Maybe even for the night."

"Oh, that wouldn't be good," Judge Ragsdale affirmed. "It gets quite cold in the mountains at night, especially at this time of year. Please, come on in."

"Thanks. Oh, could I borrow your telephone? I need to call someone about my car, and I can't seem to get a signal on my cell."

Judge Ragsdale laughed. "Oh, heavens, we don't have one of Mr. Bell's instruments out here," he said.

"You don't? How do you get by without a telephone?"

"Quite easily, actually. We have no need for such a thing. Why, whom would we talk to? I don't know anyone else who has the telephone either. But don't worry about your vehicle. There are none about who would disturb it."

Sylvia Ragsdale looked at Timmy and Christine. "Children, we will be having lunch soon. And this afternoon, we shall decorate the Christmas tree. Then tomorrow, well, what is tomorrow?" she asked.

"Tomorrow is Christmas!" Christine said excitedly.

"Indeed it is," Sylvia said. "Which means that we must decorate the tree today. Tomorrow we will have a taffy pull. I'm sure you will enjoy that."

"What's a taffy pull?" Timmy asked.

"Heavens! Do you mean to tell me you have never been to a taffy pull?"

"No, ma'am," Timmy said.

"Me neither," Christine added.

"Well, I'll just have to get Emma to tell you all about it."

"Who's Emma?" Timmy asked.

"Emma is my daughter," Sylvia explained. "She's seven years old. I think the three of you will get on quite nicely. She is somewhere here about, with the other children. Why don't we find her?" Sylvia extended her hand. Christine took it, and she and Timmy followed the judge's wife into the house.

"And while Sylvia is looking after the children, I'll show you to your room," Judge Ragsdale said, lifting two of the suitcases.

"Thank you," T. J. said and hefted the other two.

Six

T. J. and Madison followed the judge up the wide front steps, past the large, white columns on the porch, and into the house.

"Oh, what a lovely house you have," Madison said. "It is absolutely beautiful."

"Thank you," Judge Ragsdale said. "It has been in the family for a long time."

"I can see that it is a classic. Is this your home, or do you just use it as a bed-and-breakfast?"

"This is my home, and we have our bed and take our breakfast here."

Madison smiled. "Touché," she said. "I know I'm sometimes too curious. I'm sure it's the reporter in me."

"You are a court reporter?"

"No, I'm on tele—" Madison started, then she interrupted herself with a little laugh. "Judge Ragsdale, I do believe you are having fun at my expense."

They entered through a foyer where a wide, curving staircase beckoned them to the second floor. To the right of the foyer was a great room, dominated by a large Christmas tree, as yet undecorated. Several people in the great room sat on sofas or in chairs, or stood around in little conversational groups. All of them wore period costume.

"This is our keeping room," Judge Ragsdale said. "Please come join the others when you are settled in."

To the left of the foyer was a very long dining room table with twelve chairs on each side, plus one chair on either end. The table was already set with shining china, glistening silver, and sparkling crystal.

T. J. stopped and took a deep whiff. "Oh, Madison, smell that! Cinnamon, cloves, fresh-baked bread . . . oh, what a wonderful aroma!"

Madison took a deep whiff, then smiled.

"I remember these smells from when I was a small boy, visiting my grandmother," he said.

"Your room is just at the head of the stairs, on the second floor," Judge Ragsdale said. "If you'll follow me."

The polished hardwood floor of the upstairs hallway shone along each edge of the crimson runner that covered the entire length of the hall. The walls were lined with tables, chairs, and a series of potted trees. Oversized paintings hung from the picture rail, including one of a much younger Ragsdale wearing the uniform of a Confederate colonel.

"I see you are into Civil War reenacting as well," T. J. said, pointing to the painting.

"I beg your pardon?"

"That's you in a Confederate colonel's uniform, isn't it?"

"Indeed it is. Colonel of Cavalry."

"I must say, you look very striking as a Confederate Colonel," Madison said.

"Sylvia likes that portrait," Judge Ragsdale replied. "But of course she didn't know me when I had that portrait done. She was quite young then."

Judge Ragsdale pulled a watch from his pocket and, like MacLeod before him, opened the cover to look at the face. "According to my watch, it lacks fifteen minutes of twelve. You will just have time to see to your room before coming down for luncheon." He opened a door, then stepped into the room, holding out his hand in invitation. "This is our finest room. I do hope you enjoy it."

The Carmichaels stared into a room filled with beautifully preserved antiques: a dresser with a large, beveled mirror; a chifforobe; and a washstand upon which sat a porcelain basin and pitcher. At the far end of the room, a blue velvet settee and two matching chairs formed a cozy seating area in front of a fireplace. Though there was no fire at the moment, the wood had been laid, and there was a wood basket alongside with a generous supply of fuel to feed any fire they might build.

The centerpiece of the room was the bed, a beautiful canopied four-poster, which sat so high from the floor that steps were set alongside to enable one to climb in. In one corner of the room stood a tall, painted screen.

"Oh, that screen is lovely." Madison pointed. "Is it hiding something? What's behind it?"

"Come, I will show you," Judge Ragsdale replied. They followed him over to the screen and watched as he pulled it to one side to expose a large brass tub.

"It's beautiful. Where on earth did you find such a beautiful piece?"

"It was brought in from Cincinnati," Judge Ragsdale said. "It's lovely."

"When you are ready for your bath, let me know, and I shall see to it that you have hot water."

"Wait a minute," Madison said. "You mean this is functional? Not only functional, it is actually how you expect your guests to take their baths?"

"What about a bathroom?" T. J. asked.

"Oh, yes, well, I know that some establishments have a separate room set aside for bathing, but, as we so frequently have guests, I believe it is better to allow for some privacy."

"No, I mean, uh . . ."He looked at Madison, searching for some word that would stay in character.

"The necessary room," she suggested. "A privy."

"We have two privies out back," Judge Ragsdale conceded. "One for men and one for women."

"Outdoor privies," T. J. said.

"Yes, but they are quite comfortable, well-chinked against the cold wind. Oh, I see there is no water in the pitcher." Judge Ragsdale picked it up. "I'll get some; you'll want to wash up for lunch." He stepped out of the room.

"No bathroom," T. J. said quietly.

"And the bed," Madison replied. "It's not a king. It isn't even a queen. It's just a double."

"Well, I guess a king- or queen-sized bed just doesn't fit their historical motif," he said. "But to tell you the truth, if we had the car with us, I think I would just drive away."

"Yes, but we don't have the car, so we're just going to have to make the best of it.

Ragsdale returned, carrying the pitcher filled with water. "Let me know if you need more," he said.

"Thanks, Judge," T. J. said. "Oh, what about the children? Do you have roll-away beds we can put in here for them?"

"Oh, no. We'll put pallets on the floor in the keeping room, and all the children will sleep there tonight," Judge Ragsdale said. "It's great fun for them. They all enjoy it."

"Timmy might. I don't know about Christine."

"Oh, I'm sure she will like it as well. I'll tell Emma to look out for her."

"All right for now; we can play that by ear," T. J. said. "By the way, where do we go to check in?"

"Check in?"

"Yes, I called and made our reservation, but I didn't want to leave a credit card number with the answering machine. I haven't paid yet."

"Paid for what?"

"Why, for our reservations here."

Judge Ragsdale spoke plainly. "Nonsense, you are our guests. I don't charge a fare for my guests. My payment will be if you and Mrs. Carmichael enjoy your stay with us. We'll see you at luncheon." Ragsdale exited and closed the door behind him.

T. J. stared at the door for a moment, then turned to Madison. "Well, I don't understand that. What does he mean, his pay will be if we enjoy our stay?"

"It's obvious if you stop to think about it," Madison said.

"What?"

"He wants me to do a feature about Gracehall on my show.

I mean, do you have any idea how many thousands of dollars' worth of advertising that would be?"

"Yeah, I didn't think about that."

"It was the first thing that came to my mind."

"Well, what do you think? Could you do a show about Gracehall?"

"I don't like being suckered in like this. But, yes, I think I could do it." She ran her hand across the cold, smooth fireplace mantle, then smiled. "In fact, I think it might make a very good show."

"Wow, you know what just occurred to me?" T. J. said.

"What's that?"

"Music videos. I wish I had known about this place a month ago. Corey could've done 'Christmas Past' out here."

"Well, if you really think 'Christmas Past' will survive for another year—"

"I know it will," T. J. interrupted.

"Then you could still do it, and release it next year."

"Yeah, that would give it just the bump we'd need to put it back on the charts. And in the meantime we get a free Christmas vacation." He looked over at the brass bathtub. "Such as it is."

When T. J. and Madison joined the others in the keeping room, all conversation suddenly halted. Everyone looked pointedly at Madison. Their gaze was so intense that she looked down to see if she had spilled something on herself.

She saw nothing on her crimson sweater and blue jeans that warranted such scrutiny.

"Look at that woman. My word, she's wearing trousers," someone whispered.

"She's from the city," another answered. The looks of curiosity changed to smiles as everyone welcomed the new guests warmly.

At lunchtime the fourteen adults ate at the dining room table while the children ate in the kitchen. Although they all introduced themselves to T. J. and Madison, there were too many names to remember all at once.

Angus and Cora MacLeod, they had already met. And Thomas Duncan was the one to whom they had waved as they passed his farm. Thomas introduced his wife, Cynthia.

Jim and Laura Anderson sat closest to them. Two of the children belonged to them, including Betty, who at four was the youngest.

T. J. and Madison were the only ones from Nashville; in fact, they were the only ones from outside Morgan County. That surprised T. J., who had thought the attractive advertising flyer would have brought in more outsiders.

He looked at the array of down-home food: fried chicken, creamed potatoes, butter beans, and freshly baked bread. "I've been eating at too many burger joints. This is wonderful," he said.

"It is good, isn't it?" Madison affirmed.

"Would you care for some more potatoes, Mrs. Carmichael?" Sylvia asked, picking up one of the bowls and holding it toward her.

"Oh, no, thank you. Everything is delicious, and I've already eaten too much. Why, if I eat every meal like this for the whole time we're are here, I'll gain so much weight the folks at HeartNet will have a stroke. They'll be looking for someone else to do my show," she teased.

"Your show? Are you on stage?" Cora asked.

"I'm Madison Bain," Madison said.

The others looked at her in surprise.

"See here, this is rather embarrassing," Judge Ragsdale said.

"Don't be embarrassed. If you don't have cable, which you obviously don't, then there's no reason for you to have heard of me."

"I thought the two of you were married," Judge Ragsdale said.

Madison laughed. "What? We are married. What makes you think that we aren't?"

"His name is Carmichael, your name is Bain."

Madison laughed. "Oh, that's just the name I use for the show. Do you really not know who I am? Do none of you recognize me?"

"I'm afraid we don't see many shows here in Morgan County," Angus said.

"Well, I wouldn't say I'm in show business, exactly," Madison started.

"Sure you are," T. J. said.

"What do you mean by that?" Madison challenged.

"Your show is entertainment, isn't it? In fact, you have one of the highest-rated shows in the country right now."

"Well, yes, I guess if you put it that way," Madison said.

"We plan to have entertainment tonight," Judge Ragsdale said. "We'll tell stories and sing carols. Perhaps you would honor us by reading to us from the Scripture?"

"You want me to read from the Bible?" Madison asked.

"Yes," Judge Ragsdale said. "Oh, I know that many think women have no place in worship services, but I disagree with that. After all, look at the importance women played in the life of our Savior. It was a woman who brought our Lord into the world. And it was a woman who discovered the empty tomb, then spoke to the risen Christ. If women played such a role when Jesus was among us, then why should they not play an equally important role today?"

"Mama," a young girl said, coming into the dining room at that moment. "You said we were going to decorate the tree after lunch."

"Indeed I did," Sylvia said. "Have all the children finished eating? Are they ready?"

"Yes, ma'am," Emma said.

"Well, I don't know. I haven't heard from them. Children," she called. "Are you ready to decorate the tree?"

"Yes, ma'am!" a dozen young voices answered.

"Well, then, I suppose we should get started. Mr. and Mrs. Carmichael, would you like to join us?"

All the adults moved into the keeping room and took seats in order to watch the children decorate the tree.

"Oh, popcorn. I smell popcorn," Timmy said.

"Yes, we'll use popcorn on the tree."

"Popcorn on the tree?" Christine laughed. "That's funny. I never heard of that."

"Well, we'll just have to show you what to do, won't we?" Sylvia said.

Cora MacLeod and Cynthia Duncan came into the room then, carrying two large bowls of popcorn. As soon as the bowls were put down, several small hands dipped down into the popcorn.

"Now, don't eat it all," Sylvia cautioned. "Save some for the decorations."

Sylvia presented several of the children with needle and thread, then showed them how to string popcorn and holly berries to make a long, colorful rope. Then, the other half began dipping pinecones in whitewash. In the meantime, Sylvia opened a large box that was filled with cloth ornaments.

"Oh, Mrs. Ragsdale," Madison said as she saw the ornaments. "These are beautiful! Did you make them yourself?"

"Yes, over a period of several years," Sylvia said. She picked up a little calico horse. "This was the first one I ever made. I did this when I was a little girl, no older than my Emma."

"You do beautiful work," Madison said.

"Well, gents," Ragsdale said, "while the children and womenfolk are trimming the tree, suppose we go into the woods to gather some greenery and cut a Yule log."

"Oh, and John, don't forget to pick up some chestnuts," Sylvia said.

"Chestnuts, is it? All right, and while we're at it we might also collect some mistletoe." He looked at the other men and smiled. "That is, if you think we can get the ladies to stand under it long enough for a bit of sparking."

"Oh, John, how you do carry on!" Sylvia said, embarrassed. The others laughed.

"Bundle up, gents. It's a mite cold in the woods," Judge Ragsdale cautioned.

As T. J. donned his bright-yellow jacket, he felt the others looking at him.

"That's some coat you're wearing, Mr. Carmichael," one of the men said.

"Uh, yeah. I ordered it on-line about a month ago."

"You don't say," Thomas Duncan said. "Well, what will Sears and Roebuck come up with next?"

Seven

When the seven men left the house, they were well prepared for the activity ahead. Four of them carried double-headed axes, and one man pulled a sled with a two-man saw tied to it. Despite the lack of snow, the sled trailed rather easily over the carpet of leaves and pine needles. To T. J.'s surprise, Judge Ragsdale was carrying a rifle.

"Are we going hunting?" T. J. asked.

Ragsdale laughed. "Well, not for anything we can eat."

The gray sky hung threateningly above. The change in the weather surprised T. J.; it had been a bright, sunny day when they arrived.

"Boys, I do believe the children are going to get their wish," Ragsdale said. "It looks like it's going to snow."

"That's funny," T. J. said. "I checked the weather forecast before I left home. There was no snow predicted."

"Well, I don't know what prediction that was, but the *Farmers' Almanac* foretold snow for December 24," Angus MacLeod said.

"That's a fact," Anderson agreed. "I do everything by the *Almanac*."

"A fella's a fool that don't," Duncan added.

The men crossed an open field, then started up a path that led into the woods. Within a short distance, the path ascended steeply.

"You know, I've really only seen these woods from a distance," T. J. said. "This is the first time I've ever been this close. With all the red maple trees, it must be beautiful in the fall."

"Yes," Judge Ragsdale replied "And the dogwood and sourwood are pretty in the spring as well. Have you ever tasted sourwood honey?"

"No, I can't say that I have," T. J. admitted.

"Well, we have some put up. When we get back I'll have Sylvia serve us some hot biscuits with butter and sourwood honey. There's nothing better."

If anyone had asked, T. J. would have answered that he was in pretty good shape. He routinely worked out in the gym, but he found it difficult to keep up with the others, who seemed to climb effortlessly up the narrow mountain trail. He could see his breath forming vapor clouds in the frigid air.

"How much farther is it?" he finally asked.

"It's just a bit," Ragsdale said, reassuringly.

"Have pity on Mr. Carmichael, Judge. He's a city fella," Duncan said. "Maybe we should slow down a bit."

"You want to slow down, Mr. Carmichael?" Judge Ragsdale asked.

"No, I'm fine," T. J. said. "I was just curious."

They walked on for another half hour, finally reaching an open area at the top of the mountain.

"There it is." The judge pointed to a fallen tree. "I saw it here last summer and figured it would be cured just about right come Christmastime."

"What part of it do you want to take out, John?" Duncan asked.

"I've already got it measured and marked to fit the fireplace," Judge Ragsdale said. "From here to here will be just about right." He showed them the blaze marks he had cut into the tree.

The younger men started working on the tree then, two at each end of the log. The four worked in near-perfect harmony, the powerful axe blows causing the woodchips to fly.

"What do you think of the log, Mr. Carmichael?" the judge asked.

"It seems awfully big," T. J. said.

"Indeed it is big. I figure we'll light it tonight, and it will still be burning tomorrow morning."

"What are you going to do, use a power saw to cut it up more?" T. J. asked.

Judge Ragsdale laughed. "What? Take this to the mill and let them cut it up for us? No, there's no need for their powerful blade. Besides, it's a Yule log, not Yule kindling," he teased. "We'll burn it all in one piece."

The others laughed at the judge's joke.

As they continued to chop, T. J. walked over to the edge of the clearing and looked out over the range of mountains. The snow had begun falling steadily, and the tops of the trees glistened white. They were far from any interstate or other paved road, so far removed from "civilization" that it was almost as if they were on the backside of the moon.

He heard loud cheering behind him, and when he turned he saw that the cutters had done their job. The section of tree trunk Judge Ragsdale had pointed out now lay separated from the rest of the tree.

"Boys," he said ceremoniously, "behold our Yule log! Let's get it on the sled so we can take it home."

A couple of men brought up the sled, then four of them loaded the very large log.

Judge Ragsdale pulled a cloth bag from inside his coat and held it out. "Angus, if you and Thomas would go over there toward that little hollow, I think you'll find enough chestnuts to fill this bag. You other three start cutting greenery, pine boughs, and holly. Mr. Carmichael, you come with me."

T. J. followed the judge a little farther up the path.

"All that's left now is the mistletoe," Judge Ragsdale said. "And I saw some up here just the other day."

"I don't think I've ever seen mistletoe in the wild. In fact, the only time I've ever seen it at all is at somebody's Christmas party."

"Where do you think they got it?" Ragsdale asked.

"Well, I'm sure they bought it. Around Christmastime you can get it just about anywhere."

"They bought it? You mean people will pay good money for something they can just go out into the woods and harvest themselves?"

Now it was T. J.'s turn to laugh. "Judge, when you live in the middle of a city, you don't always have the opportunity to gather it for yourself."

"I suppose that's right," Ragsdale relented. "I don't really know much about city living, though I once took a train from Chattanooga down to Mobile."

"The *Chattanooga Choo Choo*," T. J. said, smiling.

"Hmm. I never heard 'em call it that, but I reckon that's what it was." The judge held up his hand. "Hold on, here we are." He looked up into the trees, then a big smile broke across his face. "Yes, sir, there it is."

"Where?" T. J. looked around in confusion.

"Up there." Judge Ragsdale pointed, his arm held at about a sixty-degree angle. "The thing about mistletoe is, it doesn't ever seem to grow close to the ground. It's about three-quarters of the way up that tree."

"Oh, yeah, I see it. It is way up there, isn't it? How are we going to get it down?"

"Why, we're going to shoot it down, of course." Ragsdale handed his rifle to T. J. "Here, you can have the first shot."

T. J. looked at the weapon, holding it stiffly. "Uh, I don't know about this. I'll be honest with you, Judge. I've never even fired a gun."

"You've never fired a gun in your entire life?" the judge asked, obviously astonished.

"I've just never been into guns."

"Well, there's nothing to it," Judge Ragsdale explained. "All you have to do is jack a round into the chamber with this lever." He pulled the lever down, then back up. "Now, see how this hammer is pulled back?"

"Yes, sir."

"Well, that means it's ready to fire. So after you put a bullet in the chamber, you should let the hammer down real easy, like this." The judge eased the hammer down, then handed the rifle to T. J.

The rifle felt awkward in T. J.'s hands. He wanted to hand it back but realized that at best it would be an admission of his inadequacy, and at worst an insult to the judge. He raised it to his shoulder.

"All right, now is the time to pull back on the hammer," the judge instructed.

T. J. thumbed the hammer back. The little metallic click echoed loudly in the silence of the woods.

"Now, what you do is look up the barrel there and put the front site in the middle of the back site, and line it up with the mistletoe. When you're ready, pull the trigger. But you want to squeeze it, not jerk on it."

Following the judge's instruction, T. J. aimed at the mistletoe, then carefully squeezed the trigger. The rifle kicked back against his shoulder, and he saw pieces of the tree limb fly away from the impact of the bullet. The gunshot echoed back from the surrounding hills in repeated volleys. When all was said and done, though, the clump of mistletoe was still there.

"You want a second shot at it?" Judge Ragsdale asked.

Sheepishly, T. J. shook his head and handed the rifle back to the judge. "No. I'd just be wasting bullets."

"Well, I'll probably miss it too," the judge said. "It's not that easy to bring down." Cocking the rifle, he raised it to his shoulder, took aim, and fired. A large clump of mistletoe fell from the branch, and it was on the ground before the last echo died away.

"You got it," T. J. said.

"Hmm. Lucky shot, I reckon."

T. J. didn't say anything, but he was pretty certain that wasn't the case.

"Let's get back and help the others gather the greenery," Ragsdale suggested.

By the time the men returned to the house, the tree was decorated with ropes of green and red yarn and the garlands of popcorn and holly berries the children had put together. Whitewashed pinecones hung amid the cloth bows and other decorations.

"All right, children, now it's time to spread the greenery around," Sylvia said. With cheers the children ran outside to bring in the pine boughs, while the men carried in the log and put it in the fireplace. Within a short time the keeping room, as well as the foyer and staircase banister, were decorated in greenery, augmented with large, red, cloth bows.

"There, now," Mrs. Ragsdale said when all was done. "Haven't the children done a good job?"

"A good job? They've done a *marvelous* job," Madison said. "I don't think I have ever seen a house more beautifully decorated."

Eight

"Bundle up for the sleigh ride!" Judge Ragsdale called from the bottom of the stairway.

Everyone had just eaten a delicious supper of potato soup, hot biscuits, butter, and sourwood honey. The kids and adults gathered around the judge.

"You're taking the children for a sleigh ride? Oh, how delightful," Madison said. "I'm sure they will enjoy that."

"Not just the children," Ragsdale replied. "Everyone is going."

"How large is the sleigh?" T. J. asked.

"Oh, don't worry about that. We have two of them," the judge said. "The grown-ups will go in one and the children in the other. There are plenty of lap robes to keep you warm, but you will be more comfortable if you are bundled up besides."

Once again, T. J. put on his bright yellow coat. Madison's coat was much like his, except that hers was lavender in color.

Everybody waited in the foyer until the two sleighs were brought around, then the judge announced that they were ready. "As you pass under the door," he said, "please look up."

The Andersons were the first ones out and, looking up, Jim saw the mistletoe. He laughed, then leaned down to kiss Laura.

Each subsequent couple kissed as they passed under the

mistletoe. When it was T. J.'s turn, he looked at Madison and hesitated for just a moment, to see how she was going to react.

"Don't be shy now," Judge Ragsdale said. "It's the rule, you know. You must kiss when you are under the mistletoe."

"What do you think?" T. J. asked.

"Don't make a scene, T. J.," Madison said quietly. "Just do it."

Madison raised her lips to T. J., and he kissed her briefly before going on outside.

The snow that had fallen earlier in the day had stopped, and the clouds had dissipated to create a clear night. The sky was filled with sparkling, crystal stars, so close that it seemed to T. J. that he could reach out and grab one. The light of the full moon reflected brilliantly off the snow.

The guests climbed into the sleighs, then placed the lap robes over their legs. The lap robes, their heavy clothing, and the close contact made it comfortably warm.

Angus drove the first sleigh; Thomas Duncan, the second.

"All right, Angus, we're all aboard," Judge Ragsdale said.

"You folks hold on!" Angus called as he snapped his whip. The team of horses got under way with bells jingling as they trotted up the lane. The sleigh slid easily through the snow, making a quiet whispering *whish* as it moved.

"Look how bright it is," Madison said. "It's almost like daytime."

"Yes, that's because of the snow and the stars and the full moon," T. J. said. He paused, and a puzzled look came over his face. "Wait a minute. That's funny."

"What's funny?"

"Last night when I took the trash out, there was no moon at all. Tonight we have a full moon. How can that be?"

"It was probably covered by a cloud."

"I suppose so."

Laura Anderson started singing "Jingle Bells," and the others in the sleigh joined her. They finished the song with laughter and self-congratulatory applause.

"I've never been on a sleigh ride before," T. J. said. "Have you?"

"No, I haven't," Madison answered. "I'm glad the kids didn't have to wait until they are as old as we are to have this experience."

T. J. turned in his seat to look at the sleigh behind them. "You think they're enjoying themselves?" he asked her.

"Are you kidding? I think they're having the time of their lives."

"You don't think they miss their PlayStation or Karaoke?"

"Amazingly enough, I don't think they miss anything," Madison said. "For that matter, they aren't even missing electricity. I think it was a good idea, our coming here like this. We're giving them a Christmas they will remember for a long time."

"In more ways than one," T. J. replied.

"What do you mean?" Then, before he could answer, Madison realized what he meant and added, "Oh."

The sleigh ride lasted for nearly an hour. They glided over white meadows and slipped along winding roads that were lined on both sides by pine trees, their boughs heavily laden with snow. The initial conversation and boisterous singing ended, to be replaced by a quiet reverence for the beauty of what they were experiencing.

Finally the party returned to Gracehall. Judge Ragsdale hopped down first, then climbed to the top step so he could address the others as they were getting out of the sleighs.

"Folks, take a few minutes to get out of your coats, sweaters, and scarves, then gather in front of the fireplace in the keeping room. We'll light the Yule log, then have freshly baked cookies, hot cider for the adults, and hot chocolate for the children. This will be the time for the singing of carols and reading of Scripture."

Following the judge's announcement, all the guests, including T. J. and Madison, went to their rooms to take off their coats and sweaters.

"We've talked about the kids enjoying this," T. J. said. "But what about you? Are you having a good time, Madison? I mean, under the circumstances."

Madison nodded. "Yes, I'm having a good time," she said. "Under the circumstances."

"I feel a little guilty though," T. J. said.

"About what?"

"We brought the kids here so we could make this last family Christmas something very special, but we've been all but ignoring them since we arrived. They're eating at a separate table, they rode in a different sleigh, and they'll be sleeping in a different room tonight. It's almost as if there is some great plan to keep them and us apart."

"I know," Madison said. "But they seem to be enjoying themselves so much with the other children that I've been hesitant to interfere."

"When do you think we should tell them about . . . ?"

"I don't know." Madison didn't want to think about it, let alone talk about it. Her feelings were mixed up now, less clear than they had been a day or two before. She wondered what T. J. was really thinking. "It's not something I'm looking forward to."

"Me neither. It's going to be hard to make them understand. I'm not sure I understand."

"T. J.," Madison started. Maybe this was the opening; maybe it wasn't too late . . .

T. J. interrupted her thought. "But we have to tell them. We can't just let it happen."

His words extinguished the little glimmer of hope Madison had just experienced.

"No, we can't just let it happen." She offered a silent prayer of desperation.

Sometime during the day, T. J. had begun to hope they could save their marriage. He wondered if they could still work it out. But he could not bring himself to say it. And Madison's words gave him no indication that she had changed her mind.

So be it. If she was determined to end their relationship, he wouldn't try to change her mind or keep her against her will. Yet . . . he could barely believe this was happening. In an effort to get his mind off this depressing subject, T. J. broke the silence. "You know what? I'm almost glad the car broke down."

"What?" she responded. "That's a strange thing to say."

"No, think about it, Madison. I mean, these people are really into this history thing. It would have been out of place to drive up in a Mercedes."

"Oh, yes, I see what you mean. It is rather amazing, isn't it? I mean the degree of authenticity everyone maintains." Madison threw herself into the conversation in order to crowd out her own maudlin thoughts. "Do you remember that time we visited the full-scale replica of the *Mayflower?* How the crew and passengers were so in character that they pretended to know nothing beyond the date they were portraying?"

"Yes. Now that you mention it, we weren't supposed to ask them anything about the Revolutionary War, or even Plymouth colony. We could ask them about nothing that happened after November 11, 1620. It's the same here."

"No, it's not the same here," Madison replied. "Those people on board the *Mayflower* replica were actors performing for the public. The difference is, here *everyone* is like that— even the guests. Except us, I mean."

"Judge and Mrs. Ragsdale live here full time. Can you imagine having to keep up their personae all the time?"

"The Amish do," Madison said.

"Yes, but they've had a lifetime of doing it. These people aren't Amish."

"No, but that does bring up a wild theory I have."

"What theory is that?"

"T. J., what if these people aren't acting? What if it's real?"

"What do you mean, real? How can it be real?"

"What if there is some little pocket of people who, like the Amish, have resisted change?"

"Are there other groups like the Amish?" T. J. asked.

"I don't know," Madison said. "But given how small and

remote this particular group is, they could have their own unique society, and the rest of the world would never even know about it."

"Sounds pretty far-fetched to me. Don't forget, they put out that slick, four-color brochure. And they took our reservation by voice mail. Whoever these people are, they haven't entirely turned their backs on technology."

"Neither have the Amish, when you think about it," she said. "Authentic Amish products, from toys to dolls to furniture, are advertised on the Internet. You can't be more modern than the Internet."

"You might be right," he agreed.

"I know I'm right," Madison said. "And as soon as I get back to Nashville, I'm going to pitch Evan the idea of doing a show about these people and this place."

"Do you really want to do that?" T. J. asked.

"Why not? I think it would make a great show. And it would advertise their business for them."

"It might also destroy their way of life," T. J. suggested. "I mean, think about it. You would do your show; other networks would pick up on it. It would go out on the five-thirty newscasts all across the country. Next thing you know, tourists would be coming in here, followed by social workers and anthropologists. These people have found a little piece of paradise. Why take it away from them?"

Before Madison could respond, there was a knock on the door. When T. J. opened it, Ragsdale was standing there with a broad smile on his face.

"We are starting the Christmas Eve festivities now. Come on down to the keeping room."

"Thanks, we'll be right there," T. J. said.

Except for one flickering candle, the keeping room was dark. It still smelled faintly of cider and cinnamon and fresh-baked cookies. T. J. and Madison picked their way carefully through the shadows, then found a place to sit. The adults as well as the children sat on the floor in a semicircle around the fireplace, wherein lay the log that the men had dragged down from the mountain.

A three-legged stool stood near the fireplace, and on the stool were a basin, a pitcher, and a towel.

Judge Ragsdale stood then and addressed the others.

"As you know, the lighting of the Yule log is one of the most important parts of Christmas. Its light symbolizes the light that the birth of Christ brought to a dark world. Let us pray."

T. J. looked around to see if the others were going to stand or kneel. When they merely bowed their heads, he did the same.

"Lord, we thank Thee now for light, for the sun by day, and for the moon, the candles, and the lanterns that push away the darkness of the night. We thank Thee for the star that guided the shepherds and the kings to the newborn Christ child. But, most especially, Lord, we thank Thee for the light Christ brought to the world, and we burn this Yule log that its light may be a symbol to us of the gift Thou didst bestow upon us that night. Amen."

"Amen," the others repeated.

"And now, Dermott, as you are the oldest male child present, would you assist me in lighting the Yule log?"

Dermott stood and walked over to the little stool. He draped the towel over his arm, then picked up the pitcher and held it. When Judge Ragsdale put his hands over the basin, Dermott poured water over them. Judge Ragsdale washed his hands, then dried them using the towel Dermott provided.

With that done, Dermott went to retrieve the candle. He carried it back to the fireplace where Judge Ragsdale was holding a charred piece of wood.

"This wood is all that is left from last year's Yule log," the judge explained. "With it, we shall light the new log, symbolizing the eternity of Christ's Kingdom."

The judge held the charred piece into the flame of the candle until it caught, then, when it was blazing well, he held it under the bark of the new log. Within a few seconds, a flame curled up around the log. The flame spread wide until soon the entire log was blazing, snapping, and popping as little trapped pockets of gas were ignited.

Sylvia and Cynthia brought in cookies, cider, and hot chocolate. Then the judge looked over at Madison.

"And now, Mrs. Carmichael, if you would please, read to us from the second chapter of St. Luke."

Madison did not have a Bible with her, and she felt a moment of awkwardness as she stood, but, smiling, the judge held one out to her. Thanking him, she cleared her throat, then turned to face the others.

As she stood before this small group of people, about to read from the Bible, she felt a sense of awe and responsibility unlike anything she had ever experienced. She began to read in a clear voice.

"And it came to pass in those days, that there went out a decree from Caesar Augustus, that all the world should be taxed.

"(And this taxing was first made when Cyrenius was governor of Syria.)

"And all went to be taxed, every one into his own city."

Madison felt the words filling up her soul. It was as if she was experiencing an answer to her hasty, almost thoughtless prayer. She read on.

"And Joseph also went up from Galilee, out of the city of Nazareth, into Judea, unto the city of David, which is called Bethlehem; (because he was of the house and lineage of David) be taxed with Mary his espoused wife, being great with child.

"And so it was, that, while they were there, the days were accomplished that she should be delivered.

"And she brought forth her firstborn son, and wrapped him in swaddling clothes, and laid him in a manger; because there was no room for them in the inn."

The children, especially, listened to the familiar story with eager innocence, drinking in every word. They gave Madison a sense of purpose and responsibility.

"And there were in the same country shepherds abiding in the field, keeping watch over their flock by night.

"And, lo, the angel of the Lord came upon them, and the glory of the Lord shone round about them: and they were sore afraid."

Madison shivered involuntarily at the thought of angels from heaven. . . .

"And the angel said unto them, 'Fear not; for, behold, I bring you good tidings of great joy, which shall be to all people.

"For unto you is born this day in the city of David a Saviour, which is Christ the Lord.

"And this shall be a sign unto you; Ye shall find the babe wrapped in swaddling clothes, lying in a manger.

"And suddenly there was with the angel a multitude of the heavenly host praising God, and saying, Glory to God in the highest, and on earth peace, good will toward men."

Finishing the reading, Madison looked up at the rapt faces of her audience. "The holy Gospel of our Lord Jesus Christ, according to St. Luke," she said.

Only T. J., Timmy, and Christine responded. "Glory to you, Lord Christ."

"Thank you, Mrs. Carmichael," Sylvia said. "You read beautifully. Now, what do you say to some carols?"

"Mama, can the first one be 'Silent Night'?" Emma asked.

"'Silent Night' it will be."

Nine

The songs, stories, and visiting ended shortly after nine o'clock, at which time Sylvia, Cora, Cynthia, and Laura spread pallets on the floor for the children.

"Timmy, Christine, do you want to come to our room?" Madison invited.

"No," the boy answered. "Everyone would laugh at us. Besides, I think it will be fun to be down here with all the other kids."

"What about you, Christine?"

"I want to stay with my new best friend," she said.

Madison smiled. "And who would that be?"

"Emma is my best friend in the whole world."

"Oh? What about Lauren? Don't you think she might be upset if she thinks she isn't your best friend anymore?"

"She's my best friend too," Christine said. "Lauren and Emma are both my best friends."

"That's dumb," Timmy said. "You can't have two best friends."

"Yes, you can, if your heart is big enough," Christine insisted. "Mama loves Daddy, you, and me all the same because her heart is big enough. Isn't that true, Mama?"

Madison hesitated for a moment. Looking across the room, she saw T. J. talking to Angus MacLeod.

"Isn't that true, Mama?" Christine asked again.

"Yes, darling, that's true," Madison said.

"See there?" The girl turned triumphantly to her brother. "Mama said I can too have two best friends. So, may I stay down here, Mama?"

"Yes, if you want to."

"I'm going to go make sure my bed is close to Emma's." Christine ran happily to find her friend, almost knocking Timmy over as she went.

"Mom, are you and Dad having fun?" Timmy asked.

Madison was surprised and somewhat disconcerted by Timmy's question. She looked down at him standing there, his face upturned. "What?" she replied.

"It doesn't seem like you and Dad . . . well, you know . . . you don't seem like you ever have much fun anymore. I just wanted to know if you are having fun now."

"Well, sweetheart, the important thing is for you and Christine to have fun. Christmas is supposed to be for children, not adults."

"But isn't Jesus for adults?" Timmy asked.

"Yes, of course."

"Then that means Christmas is for everybody, doesn't it?"

"You're right, son. Christmas is for everyone."

"Do you know what I want for Christmas, more than any other thing?"

Madison chuckled. "Oh my, it's Christmas Eve already. Don't you think it's a little late to be adding to your wish list?"

"Not if you are asking God for it. It's never too late to ask God for something, is it?"

Madison was taken aback. The family so rarely went to

church these days; they had drifted away over the past couple of years. But he must be listening and learning a lot at school. She was happy about that, but felt guilty at the same time. Shouldn't the parents be the first and best Christian teachers, by word and example?

"No, honey, it's never too late to ask God for something. What are you asking for?"

"I'm asking Him to make this the best Christmas you and Dad have ever had."

"Well, sweetheart, any Christmas that we're with you and Christine is a wonderful Christmas."

"No, Mom, I don't mean with Christine and me. I mean you and Dad. Together. Are you having a good time?"

"Yes, dear. We are having a good time."

Timmy smiled broadly. "I'm glad. Now I'm going to go find Dermott."

Grateful for the change of subject, Madison tried to lighten the moment. "Is Dermott your new best friend?"

Timmy laughed and wrinkled his nose. "He's not my 'best' friend, but I like him. He's really neat, Mom. He can do more things than just about anybody I know. Did you know he can stand on his hands?"

"Well now, that's quite an accomplishment, isn't it?"

"It sure is. Nobody in my class can do it. I'll bet nobody in all of Belle Meade Academy can do that."

"Well, you have a good time with your friends tonight," Madison said. "Don't get into any trouble, and keep an eye on Christine. She's your little sister, and I'm depending on you to watch out for her."

"Okay," Timmy said, hurrying across the room to find Dermott.

Madison grew pensive as she stood there alone. Did Timmy suspect the real reason for their coming here for Christmas? Did he know what Madison and T. J. were considering? They had been very careful not to say anything in front of the children, but she knew that kids were smart, and much more intuitive than adults generally gave them credit for.

She wished now that Timmy had not shared his Christmas wish, or more accurately, his Christmas prayer with her. It was going to make what had to be done much harder to carry out.

Then she caught herself and thought: What *has* to be done? Why does it have to be this way?

T. J. came up to her then. "You look lost in thought," he said.

"Oh, I, uh, was just talking with the kids."

"Are they satisfied with the sleeping arrangements?"

"More than satisfied. They're absolutely insistent. What were you talking to Mr. MacLeod about?"

"I asked if he would take me back to the car so I could get the kids' presents."

"Oh, T. J., no! You left the kids' presents in the car?"

"Yes. I'm sorry. It's just, well, with everything that was going on, I forgot."

"I don't know why I'm blaming you; I didn't think about it either. Well, what did Mr. MacLeod say? Will he take you back to the car?"

"He said he would, but he also told me that none of the guests ever bring presents. It seems that Judge Ragsdale and his wife have a history of providing gifts for all the children."

"Oh, but that's not right. He shouldn't have to do that. At least, not unless we pay him for them."

"I suggested that too, but Mr. MacLeod said that if I did that, the judge would be offended. Evidently a very big part of the judge's enjoyment at Christmas comes from giving gifts to the children."

"Well, that's very sweet of him."

"Anyway, I don't think they are going to be all that expensive. I mean, he's not likely to give a laptop or a DVD player, now is he?"

Madison smiled at his gentle sarcasm. This was the T. J. she knew—and loved? "I wouldn't think so."

"And that's another reason I think I'll just let things stand as they are. If we gave them their presents here, what they got would be vastly different from what the other children are getting. I think they might be embarrassed."

"You mean as in, 'Look at that woman. My word, she's wearing trousers.' Is that the kind of embarrassment you're talking about?"

"Yeah, something like that," T. J. said with a chuckle.

Madison looked around the room then and saw that all the adults had left, as well as the children. "What time is it? Nobody seems to be around down here."

T. J. looked at his watch. "Why, no wonder," he said. "It's a quarter till ten. Excuse me. In keeping with the theme, perhaps I should say it lacks fifteen minutes of ten."

Madison laughed. "And we're still up? My, doesn't that make us night owls?"

T. J. smiled. "Obviously, the only night owls."

The keeping room had been darkened by the extinguishing of candles and lanterns. The only light now was the flickering orange of the still-burning Yule log. From the pallet area could be heard the whispers and giggles of the children as they settled in for the night.

When T. J. and Madison went upstairs, they found their room to be much colder than it had been down in the parlor. But with the wood already laid, it took only a few minutes to get a fire going. Alongside the fireplace stood a scuttle filled with more wood to replenish the fire as necessary. There was also a wedge-shaped piece of metal, attached to the end of a long pole.

"I wonder what that strange-looking contraption is," T. J. said.

"It's a bed warmer," Madison explained. "You heat this thing up, then you pass it under the covers until the sheets and blankets are warm."

"I'll be doggoned, I think you're right," T. J. said as he studied it closely.

"I know I'm right. And if you'd go into an antique store now and then, you would know what it is too."

"I hate shopping."

"You hate shopping? Now, there's a revelation. On those rare occasions when I've managed to get you into a mall, you've had the expression of someone who was wearing a hair shirt."

"You think this thing really works?" He picked up the bed warmer again.

"I'm sure it does. They wouldn't have made so many of them if they didn't work."

"Okay, what do you say I warm the bed up for you?" He held the warmer out over the fire.

"What do you mean, warm the bed for me? You don't need it warmed?"

"Well, I thought . . . uh, under the circumstances, I thought I'd pull the chair up next to the fireplace and sleep there tonight."

"Oh, don't be silly, T. J. You won't get any rest sleeping in a chair."

"I can try," T. J. said. "As you pointed out, this is just a double bed, and not even a very large one at that. It might be difficult for us."

"I'm sure we can handle it."

She watched as T. J. held the warmer over the fire, studying the expression on his face, trying again to determine what he was thinking about.

"T. J.?"

"Yes?"

Madison drew a deep breath. She was about to tell him about Timmy's Christmas wish, but couldn't find the courage. Instead she said, "I think it's warm enough now."

T. J. passed the bed warmer under the covers until the chill had been taken out, then he and Madison climbed into bed. They lay with their backs to each other, clinging to the edges and making every effort not to invade each other's space.

"Good night," T. J. said.

"Good night."

T. J. lay there, watching the fire shadows dance on the wall. *I wonder if I should kiss her good night? I mean, I did kiss her under the mistletoe today. It wouldn't mean anything, just a little symbol of goodwill between us. But I'm afraid it would just make things more difficult.*

On her side of the bed, Madison stared through the window. Just outside their room was a towering pine tree, its boughs, like the boughs of all the other trees, laden with snow. The snow shimmered under the full moon, so that the tree was glowing, as if from some inner light. *I wonder if he's thinking of kissing me good night? A kiss would be nice, but it could also be misleading.*

The two of them lay stiffly in bed, struggling with the doubts that tumbled through their heads. In the fireplace, the burning wood popped and snapped. Outside their window, the boughs of the tree creaked and groaned under the weight of the snow. From somewhere nearby, an owl hooted.

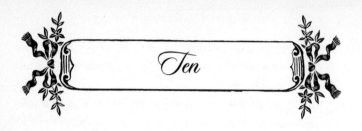

Ten

Christmas Day

"Rise and shine, everybody! This is the day of our Savior's birth! Merry Christmas to all!"

Judge Ragsdale walked along the upstairs hallway, calling out his greetings and rousing the sleeping household.

"Breakfast in one-half hour!" he called.

As T. J. and Madison awakened, they discovered that during the night, whether by necessity of position, or seeking more warmth, they had come together. Madison was lying with her back spooned against him. T. J.'s arm was draped over her shoulder, and she had embraced his arm.

For a moment they lay there, enjoying the warmth and ease of lying together in a comfortable bed. Then, in a simultaneous realization of what they were doing, they moved abruptly to pull away from each other.

"I'm sorry," he apologized. "I didn't mean to crowd you."

"That's all right," she replied. "I think we just crowded into each other."

Sliding out of bed, T. J. hurried over to the fire and tossed on several more pieces of wood. Soon the fire was again blazing cheerfully and radiating enough heat to take the chill out of the room. They dressed quickly, carefully staying on opposite sides of the bed and affording each other the privacy of the moment. When both were ready, they went downstairs.

"Mom! Dad! Look what we have!" Timmy said, bringing some of his toys over to display, with Christine at his side. "I didn't know what all of them were, but Dermott told me."

"Well, show us what you have," T. J. said.

"This is called a cup and ball," Timmy explained. "See, this ball has a string tied to it, and there's a cup on the end of this stick. What you do is, you swing the ball out, then you catch it in the cup."

Timmy tried to demonstrate. "Well, it's hard when you first try it," he said. "But Dermott can do it real easy."

"Dermott sounds like quite a lad," T. J. said.

"He is." Timmy tried again to catch the ball in the cup and failed again. "Dermott says that if you do it a whole lot of times, it gets easier." He tried it once more, and this time he was successful. "I did it! See?"

"If you keep that up, the next thing you know you'll be getting a ball-and-cup scholarship to Vanderbilt. Then, you'll make All-Southeast Conference ball-and-cup team, and you'll be drafted by the National Ball-and-Cup League. Then you'll play in the Ball-and-Cup Super Bowl. After that, you'll start getting endorsements—why, I wouldn't be at all surprised if you didn't wind up on the side of a Wheaties box."

Timmy started laughing halfway through T. J.'s spiel. "Dad, remember what I told you? Sarcasm does not become you."

"What, you mean you don't believe me? Well, maybe I was exaggerating a little. The National Ball-and-Cup League doesn't actually play a Super Bowl."

Timmy laughed again.

Madison turned to Christine, who was holding her gifts. "Show us what you got, honey."

"I got this doll. I named her Britney because she's so pretty. She's got a glass face."

"That's called bisque," Madison said.

"Biscuit?"

"Bisque. It's a type of porcelain." She examined the doll. "T. J., do you have any idea how valuable this doll is?"

"I don't know, what? Fifty, sixty dollars, maybe?"

"Try a thousand dollars," Madison said.

"What? No way. One thousand dollars?"

"At least. I did a show on antique dolls a couple of months ago, and I was amazed at how expensive some of these dolls can be. We can't let Judge Ragsdale give her something like this."

"Maybe it isn't an antique," T. J. suggested.

"Of course it is. Nobody makes dolls like this anymore."

"Well, antique or not, he seems to have given one to every little girl here," T. J. said. "If we make Christine give her doll back, might that not cause trouble with the other children?"

"Mama, you aren't going to make me give Britney back, are you?" Christine clutched the doll anxiously.

Madison looked at the doll, then at the other little girls, then back at Christine. With a sigh, she relented.

"You can keep her."

"Thanks, Mama," Christine said happily.

"Don't thank me, thank Judge Ragsdale."

"I tried to," Christine said, "but he said the toys all came from Santa Claus."

"He said that?" T. J. was surprised.

"Well, he said they came from Saint Nicholas, but isn't Saint Nicholas the same thing as Santa Claus?"

"As a matter of fact, I believe you're right," Madison said.

In addition to the cup and ball, Timmy had a game of checkers and a box of pickup sticks. Christine also received a game of "graces," hoops and wands included.

As the children were playing with the gifts Saint Nicholas had left them, breakfast was called.

The hungry group gathered yet again around the table for a country feast the likes of which T. J. and Madison had rarely seen. Madison reached for a biscuit topped with butter and sorghum molasses.

"I'm going to be 300 pounds by New Year's," she muttered to T. J., hoping no one else had heard her.

"Sorghum is a little stronger than Log Cabin syrup, isn't it?" T. J. teased, when he saw Madison's reaction to the rather pungent taste.

"I don't know that I've ever really tasted sorghum molasses," she said.

"My grandma served it all the time," T. J. explained. "I like it, but you do have to acquire the taste."

After breakfast the children returned to their toys. The adults were enjoying coffee in the keeping room when Emma walked in.

"Can we have the taffy pull now?" she asked.

"Taffy pull? Taffy pull? Who said anything about a taffy pull?" Sylvia teased.

"You did!" several young voices responded in unison.

"Oh, my! If all of you say so, then I must have mentioned it. Very well, I suppose we should get started then, shouldn't we? Mr. and Mrs. Carmichael, have either of you ever experienced a taffy pull?"

"I haven't," T. J. admitted.

"Nor have I," Madison added.

"Then you are very welcome to join us," Sylvia invited.

T. J. and Madison followed Sylvia into the kitchen where the children, from four-year-old Betty Anderson to twelve-year-old Dermott Duncan, gathered around the stove, a big iron wood-burner.

"Oh, look at that stove," Madison said quietly to T. J. "Have you ever seen one of these before—other than in pictures?"

"Sure, my grandmother had one," T. J. said.

"She did? T. J., you were born in the late fifties. Are you telling me that you can remember your grandmother using one of these?"

"Not all the time," T. J. said. "It had belonged to my great-grandmother, and my grandmother used it for baking. She said it was better than gas or electric. And as I think back on how delicious her pies and cakes were, I can't argue with her."

"All right, children, here's what we do," Sylvia explained. "We mix water, sugar, butter, and a little bit of vinegar into a sauce pan."

"Vinegar? Oh, vinegar doesn't taste good," said Betty.

"We don't put enough in to make it taste bad," Sylvia said. "We use just a little bit."

"My, look at all that sugar," Madison said, as she saw Sylvia preparing the mixture. "That can't be good for the children."

"Oh, but it is good. They love it. Wait until you taste it; you'll like it too."

"No, I meant, it can't be healthy for them."

"What a strange thought. They're children. You don't have to worry about children being healthy!"

Sylvia held the pot over the stove lid, then moved it off and put it back on several times, explaining that she didn't want it to overheat. When the sugar was completely dissolved, she cooked it a while longer, then dipped out a teaspoonful of the mixture.

"Let's see if it is ready." She poured the liquid into a glass of water, where it immediately formed into a ball.

"All right, my part is done," she said, pouring the mixture onto a buttered platter. "Now it's up to you children to finish it."

"Yea!" Emma said.

The children, including Timmy and Christine, greased their hands with butter, then, as soon as Sylvia determined it was cool enough to touch, broke pieces off and began pulling and stretching. Even T. J. and Madison got into the act, buttering their own hands and pulling on opposite ends of the same piece of taffy. Surrounded by the children's squeals of delight and the warmth of the kitchen, T. J. and Madison were absorbed in the moment.

When the taffy had been pulled into several rope-shaped pieces, Sylvia announced that it was ready to take outside and put on the snow to cool.

"If you listen, you'll hear it pop and crack, like icicles breaking off the trees and falling in the woods," Sylvia explained.

"We're going to go outside and listen," Emma said.

"You all can listen if you want to," Dermott said. "I'm going to play with my new sled."

"Oh, Mom, can I go outside too?" Timmy asked.

"Me too? Can I go outside?" Christine pleaded.

"All right, you may go, but bundle up," Madison said. "I don't want you two coming down with the flu."

Emma laughed. "That's funny," she said.

"What's funny?" Madison asked.

"I've heard of Saint Nicholas coming down the chimney, but I've never heard of boys and girls coming down the flue," she said, giggling.

The other children laughed as well.

"Mama, what's a flue?" Christine asked.

"Well, it's, uh . . . ask your father."

"Dad, what's a flue?" Timmy asked.

"Don't you know what a flue is?" Emma interrupted. "It's where the stovepipe connects to the chimney so the smoke doesn't get in your house."

"Yeah, that," T. J. said.

Minutes later, when T. J. and Madison were up in their room washing the butter from their hands, Madison started to laugh.

"What is it?" T. J. asked. "Why are you laughing?"

"'Yeah, that,'" Madison mimicked. "You didn't know what a flue was either!"

"Sure I did. I told you, my grandmother had one of those old stoves. And it had a stovepipe that went to one of those . . . thingees."

"Thingees?"

"Yeah, well, I've seen them. I just didn't know what they were called."

Madison splashed water on him.

"Hey! Stop that!"

She did it again.

"Okay, two can play that game." He picked up the water basin.

"No, no!" Madison said, holding her hands up in front of her. "T. J., be careful with that. Do you have any idea how old it is? It would be awful if you broke it."

"All right, all right, I guess you've outsmarted me again."

Madison stepped over to the door, then smiled at him. "Outsmarting you isn't such a big accomplishment . . ."

T. J. picked up a pillow and threw it at her, but hit only a shut door.

As he returned the pillow to the bed, he realized that this was the first time he and Madison had bantered in a long, long time. He liked the feeling.

While the children played outside, the adults gathered in the keeping room.

"Now, folks," the judge announced, "if I can prevail upon Sylvia to play the piano for us, I suggest we have a musicale, with everyone taking a turn to sing us a song."

"Sing a song? You mean, individually?" Madison asked.

"Yes, it'll be great entertainment," the judge replied. Sylvia walked over to the piano and sat down.

"Now, wait a minute, John," Thomas Duncan said. "You might remember that when I sang last year, you said I sounded like—what was the phrase you used?"

Cynthia laughed. "I think he said you sounded like a heifer bawling because her foot was hung up in a barbed-wire fence."

The others laughed.

"That's what he said, Thomas," Angus said. "And he was right, too."

"There. Now, remembering that, do you still want me to sing?"

"I do, indeed," Judge Ragsdale insisted. "Part of the fun will be in listening to the bad as well as the good. For only by going into the valley can you enjoy the peaks."

"We promise not to throw chairs at you, Thomas," Jim Anderson said, and again the others laughed.

"I wish Corey were here," T. J. said. "He could do the singing for all of us."

"Who is Corey?" Sylvia asked. "A relative of yours?"

"I'm talking about Corey Doolin. He's one of my clients."

When T. J. got no response, he said Corey's name again. "Corey Doolin."

T. J. got nothing but blank stares from the others.

"Come on, don't tell me that none of you have ever heard of Corey Doolin. 'Ruby Lips'? 'Christmas Past'? You've never heard of those songs?"

As the others looked at each other in absolute confusion, T. J. glanced over at Madison, his own face a mask of exasperation. "I guess they aren't country music fans," he whispered.

Madison chuckled. "Now you know how I felt yesterday

when no one had heard of me," she replied quietly. "Welcome to Ego Reality Check 101."

T. J. addressed the others. "I just can't believe . . ." he started, then, as if thinking about something else, he stopped in midsentence and smiled. "All right, if you don't know who he is, it's not too late to find out. Corey Doolin is a singer, and a very good one. He is one of the most popular singers in America. 'Ruby Lips,' 'Waiting for You,' and 'Christmas Past' are three of his greatest hits. Right now they are selling more CDs and getting more airplay than all the other songs out there."

T. J. reached into his pocket and pulled out the golden treble clef brooch. He stepped over to the piano to hand the piece to Sylvia. "Here," he said. "Merry Christmas."

Sylvia examined the jeweled brooch for a moment, then quickly handed it back, almost as if it had burned her fingers.

"I can't take this," she said.

"What?" T. J. asked, surprised by her reaction. "What do you mean? It's my Christmas gift to you."

"Oh, no, this is far too valuable a gift," Sylvia insisted.

T. J. said, "Well, I'm giving away trade secrets here, but it isn't as valuable as you think. Anyway, I have a bunch of them to give away. Do you see this ruby? That's to remind people of Corey's song, 'Ruby Lips.' It's called promotion, so if you wear this, you will actually be doing me a favor."

"It is lovely," Sylvia said, weakening somewhat as she examined it. She looked up at the judge.

"Go ahead, Sylvia," Judge Ragsdale said. "I think it will look very pretty on you."

A wide smile spread across Sylvia's face. "All right!" she said. "I'll wear it, and proudly. Thank you very much, Mr. Carmichael." She pinned the jewelry to her blouse, then showed it off to the other women who came up for a closer examination.

"I wish I had brought enough for everyone," T. J. said quietly to Madison.

"Why? If they are as isolated as we believe them to be, you wouldn't get much promotional value from the gifts."

"I don't care about that. I just think it would be nice to give them all something."

"Why, T. J.," Madison said, holding his arm and leaning into him. "I never knew you were such a softhearted soul."

"Maybe if you'd stick around a bit longer you would find out other things about me you never knew before," T. J. suggested.

She silently held his arm, experiencing a feeling that was different, yet familiar. At that moment she knew she didn't want anything to come between them or ruin their marriage. The love of the season and the day welled up within her.

Sylvia had turned her attention back to the piano. "Now, who will be first to sing for us?" she asked.

"I'll go first," Laura Anderson said.

"Are you ready for this?" T. J. whispered to Madison.

"Shh. Be nice, now," Madison whispered back.

Laura began singing "It Came upon a Midnight Clear." To T. J.'s surprise, her voice was sweet and clear. Almost involuntarily, he reached over to put his arm around Madison, pulling her close to him.

"Listen to this," he said in awe.

"It's beautiful," Madison replied.

"You know who her voice reminds me of?"

"Charlotte Church." It was an answer, not a question.

Laura finished the song to the applause of all in the room.

"I wonder if Laura would be interested in a music career," T. J. said to Madison. "I'd love to sign her."

"No," Madison replied.

"What do you mean, no? She could make a fortune."

"Don't do it, T. J."

"Why not?"

"For the same reason you asked me not to do a television show about these people. If Laura became famous, do you think for one minute some enterprising reporter wouldn't find out about her background? The next thing would be an exposé of this unique and isolated culture. If that happens, all this is gone."

T. J. took Madison's hand in his, patting it gently. "It's a shame that the world is going to be deprived of such a beautiful voice, but you're right. I couldn't be a party to destroying what they have here."

The others persuaded Laura to sing a couple more songs, making it obvious to T. J. and Madison that her talent was genuinely appreciated. Laura was followed by Cora MacLeod, who wasn't bad. Then came Thomas Duncan. T. J. decided that Thomas had been right in resisting the invitation to sing. He wouldn't quite compare the attempt at singing with the sound of a bawling heifer, but listening was somewhat of an ordeal.

After Thomas, it was Angus's turn, and he had just stepped up to the piano to offer his own musical effort when shouts were heard from the children. The room emptied as the grown-ups rushed outside.

Eleven

The children were staring at Dermott, who was floating in the cold water. Jim Anderson already was hurriedly swimming to Dermott.

"How did it happen?" T. J. asked his son.

Timmy pointed to the rotating waterwheel. "Dermott climbed up to the top and did a handstand on that wheel. He said he was going to ride it all the way down to the bottom, then jump off. But as soon as he did the handstand, he slipped and fell."

"He hit his head," one of the other children said.

Thomas and Judge Ragsdale met Jim at the water's edge and took Dermott from him. Thomas laid the boy on the dry ground while the judge examined him.

Jim, now dripping wet and shivering, watched anxiously. "How is he?" he asked.

Ragsdale held his hand under Dermott's nose, then leaned over to put his ear on Dermott's chest. He shook his head.

"He's not breathing and his heart's not beating," he said.

"No!" Cynthia, Dermott's grandmother, screamed. She began crying uncontrollably.

"No . . ." T. J. said to Madison. Suddenly, T. J. pushed his way closer to the boy, dropped to his knees, and ripped open Dermott's shirt. Then, tilting the boy's head back, he pinched

Dermott's nose, and, covering the boy's mouth with his own, blew until he could see Dermott's chest rise.

"What is he doing?" Cynthia cried.

"Please, Mrs. Duncan, everyone, T. J. knows CPR."

T. J. put both hands on Dermott's chest, and began pressing it in rhythm. "Madison, help me," he said. "Give him mouth-to-mouth after every fifteen compressions!"

Madison knelt beside T. J. and began counting.

"One, two, three, four, five, six, seven, eight, nine, ten, eleven, twelve, thirteen, fourteen, fifteen!"

T. J. stopped the chest compressions, and Madison began to administer mouth-to-mouth.

"Two times, at two seconds each!" T. J. said. "One thousand one, one thousand two!"

Madison pulled away from Dermott and took a deep breath, then bent over him again.

By now, everyone stood around watching in awed silence. T. J. and Madison continued the CPR through several cycles until suddenly Dermott coughed, and water spurted from his mouth.

"We've got him!" Madison shouted. "Oh, T. J., he's okay!" Madison stood up, and T. J. turned Dermott over, then lifted his waist so that Dermott's head hung down.

"Oh, Lord in heaven, you've brought him back to life!" Cynthia said, her expression a mixture of thankfulness and awe.

"Simple CPR," Madison said.

All attention turned to Dermott who said, "Grandma, I'm cold," and began shivering uncontrollably.

"We'll get you warmed up right now." Cynthia wrapped

him in a blanket and took him inside, followed by the others.

"You were wonderful," Madison said, embracing T. J.

"Thanks," he said. "You weren't so bad yourself."

"Folks," Judge Ragsdale said, holding his hand up to get everyone's attention. "Folks, would you all bow your heads so we may offer the Lord a prayer of thanksgiving?"

The room grew quiet as all bowed their heads. Judge Ragsdale began to pray.

"Almighty God and heavenly Father, we give Thee thanks that Thou were pleased to deliver from the clutches of death this child, on whose behalf we bless and praise Thy name. We are grateful for Mr. Carmichael's intervention to save this precious life. We pray, O Lord, that through Thy help, Dermott will live in this world according to Thy will, serving his fellow man to Thy glory, through Jesus Christ our Lord. Amen."

"Amen," the others added. With tears in their eyes, they shook T. J.'s hand and patted him on the shoulder, and hugged Madison, who stood beside him.

While Dermott and Jim left to put on warm, dry clothes, the children and grown-ups stayed behind. Laura began singing a hymn, and the others alternately joined in and quietly listened to her.

Laura's voice was so beautiful, the words of adulation and praise for the Lord so inspiring that it filled the room with an aura of worship that rivaled that of any church T. J. or Madison had ever attended.

When the music finally ended, everyone drifted away, leaving T. J. and Madison alone for a moment.

"I wonder if the judge has any boots we could wear," T. J. asked.

"Boots?"

"Yes. We didn't come prepared for the snow, but I'd like to take a walk if you'll go with me."

"Are you serious?" Madison looked at him as if he were a stranger. "I used to try to get you to take a walk with me, but you never wanted to go."

"I want to go now," he said. "What about you?"

"Well, yes, I'd love to go for a walk."

The judge did have boots, and they fit T. J. and Madison as perfectly as if they had bought them for themselves.

"We'll eat around four," the judge said as the pair left.

"We'll be here," T. J. said, smiling. "I've been smelling the cooking all day. It's driving me mad, and one reason I want to go for a walk is to keep me from going into the kitchen and start sampling."

Ragsdale laughed. "Anyway, I think it will be good for the two of you to take a nice long walk together. Long walks have a way of allowing people to see things more clearly."

T. J. and Madison stepped outside, then strolled down to the end of the brick sidewalk where they found themselves ankle-deep in the white stuff.

"Did you have anyplace special you wanted to go?" Madison asked. "Or did you just want to walk?"

"Both," T. J. said. "I want to walk, but I also want to show you where we were yesterday when I went with the men to get the Yule log."

"How far is it?"

"It's some distance. We don't have to go, but if you think you're up to it, it's worth the effort. The view is spectacular."

"I'm up to it," she answered.

They walked on in silence for several minutes, breathing hard with the effort. Clouds of white vapor curled about their noses and mouths. Finally, Madison spoke.

"T. J., what do you think Judge Ragsdale meant by that remark he made just as we left?"

"What remark?"

"He said that long walks have a way of allowing people to see things more clearly."

"I'm sure he meant nothing by it. It's probably just some homespun wisdom."

"You haven't been talking to him, have you?"

T. J. looked questioningly at Madison. "Talking to him about what?"

"About our . . . problem," Madison said.

T. J. shook his head. "No, Madison," he replied. "I've spoken to nobody about our 'problem,' as you put it. What is going on between us right now is just between us."

They walked on in silence, except for the crunching sound their boots made in the brilliant white snow. In the distance, they heard a crow's caw. The hammering of a woodpecker echoed through the woods.

"Have you ever experienced such peace?" T. J. asked.

"No, never."

"What *is* our problem, Madison?" T. J. asked. "What has gone wrong between us?"

"Are you sure you want to go there right now?"

"Yes. I'm sure."

Madison didn't answer.

"Madison, please. Talk to me."

"We don't have time for each other anymore," Madison said. "Both of us have high-pressure, high-profile, very demanding jobs. A person has only so much to give, and we are giving more of ourselves to our jobs than we are to each other."

"Other successful people manage to make marriage work," T. J. insisted. "I don't know why we can't."

"You said it yourself. One of us would have to give up his—or her—career. In fact, you were quite specific about which one of us it should be."

"I know I said that, but I was wrong. Madison, you are a wife, mother, and a career woman. As a matter of fact, you are a very successful career woman, and I should never have suggested that you give that up."

"Well, there you have it then," Madison said. "We're back where we started. We don't have time for our jobs, kids, and each other. But neither of us wants to give up the career."

"I remember that when I first met you I was drawn to you because you were so pretty and smart. I still think you are pretty . . . no, I think you are beautiful. And nobody that I know has a bigger heart than you do."

Madison smiled softly, warmly. "Christine has a big heart," she said. "Timmy too."

"What?"

"It's just some things that they've said to me recently. Christine told me today that her heart was big enough to have two best friends, just like my heart was big enough to love you, Timmy, and her, equally."

"Christine is a smart girl," T. J. said.

"T. J., I . . ." Madison started, but T. J. interrupted her.

"I want to hear it from you, Madison. I want you to tell me when you realized that you no longer loved me."

Madison gasped slightly, then looked up at him. Her eyes were glistening with tears. "What? Oh, T. J., I never said that I don't love you anymore."

"You mean you still do?"

"Love isn't like a light switch. You can't just turn it on and off."

"I think we've been here too long. What's a light switch?"

Madison laughed out loud. "Well, maybe that's not such a good analogy."

"So what you are saying is, you still love me."

"Yes, T. J. I still love you. I just don't know if that love is enough."

"You're right. Love all by itself isn't enough. But I'm willing to provide whatever is needed to nurse that love. Understanding, time for togetherness . . . whatever it takes, I'm willing to do."

"We can't just talk about this, T. J. It's going to take a lot of sacrifices—and prayer—and faith—to get this marriage back on track."

"I think it's worth it," T. J. said.

"I do too."

"All right. Where do we start?"

"Well, we'll have to—" Madison began, then she stopped. "T. J., when we were on our way here, while we were still on the interstate, we passed a little village that was down in the valley. I know this is going to sound silly, but I found myself fantasizing that we were living there as ordinary people, with ordinary jobs that let us come home every night."

"Whoa. That's . . . that's quite a start," T. J. said. "I mean, that would require a complete life change."

Madison waved him off. "No, I'm not saying let's do that. I know it was just a fantasy. But there was one part of the fantasy that we could do."

"What's that?"

"I saw a beautiful little church there. It was white, with a tall steeple. I don't even know what the denomination was, but I know this. There was something immensely comforting in thinking about attending that church, or any church, on a regular basis. That's where we could start, T. J. I think we have let our lives get out of hand, but if we can find time to bring Jesus into our lives, that will give us the structure we need to find time for each other."

"You want to start going to church on a regular basis? All of us, you and me and the kids?"

"Yes, I do."

"Like we used to, when we were first married."

"But I don't want you to do it for me, T. J. I want you to do it for the Lord, and for yourself. So don't just tell me you will unless you are serious."

"I am serious." T. J. smiled. "Did you know I used to be an acolyte—a very long time ago?"

Madison laughed. "No, I didn't."

"I enjoyed it. And I remember the comfort I got from having the Lord as a part of my life. I don't know when, or how, I let that all go. I was trying to remember that the other day, when I first heard about this place. Hey, I'll do it, and not just for you. I'll do it because I want to."

"If we go back to church together—as a family—then that will be the first step in organizing our lives along the things that are most important to us."

"We'll go to church next Sunday, as a family," T. J. promised. "And we'll eat dinner together—"

"And not take-out," Madison said. "I mean, we have that big, beautiful kitchen that we designed and seldom use."

"Hey, I'm not a bad cook myself, you know."

"No, you're not," Madison agreed. "All right, we'll share the cooking."

By now they had reached the top of the climb, and they stood there for a moment while they caught their breaths.

"We're here," T. J. said. "This is what I wanted you to see." He positioned her at the edge of the clearing, then pointed. "Have you ever seen a more magnificent sight?"

The mountains lay before them in gently rolling waves, mottled with white snow and dark color: green up close, then blue, and finally, purple for the most distant vistas. And, hanging over it all were the wisps of cloud and mist that so resembled smoke from home fires that it caused the first explorers to give the Smoky Mountain range its name.

"Oh, it is so beautiful," Madison said.

"Look. For as far as you can see, there is not one interstate, electric transmission tower, or power station to mar the view."

"T. J., you're right. There's no way I can do a story on these people. I couldn't live with myself if I did something to take this away from them."

"I know."

"This isn't just wishful thinking, is it? I mean, can we really make this marriage—this family—work?"

"Come over here," he said. "There's something else I want you to see."

"What could be more beautiful than this view?"

"Come." T. J. took her hand. He led her over to a towering tree, then pointed up. "Look up there."

"What am I looking for?"

"That's where we got the mistletoe." He pointed to the little clump of parasitic growth and smiled. "And right now you are standing directly under it."

Madison looked at him, and her eyes issued the invitation that had been missing from their marriage for a long time. "Oh, T. J."

She felt his arms reach around her and his mouth close on hers so that she mumbled the name into his breath. As T. J. pulled her to him, she grew limp.

It had been a long time since they shared a moment of this intensity. It wasn't the kiss of a husband and wife jaded by familiarity. This was the kiss of young lovers still excited over each other.

There was no rush-hour traffic, no TV show deadlines, no contract negotiations, no single-parent P.T.A. meetings, no warmed-over take-out meals, no voice-mail messages explaining missed appointments. For this moment it was just the two of them, alone in the universe. They were Adam and Eve in God's own Garden of Eden. And Madison wished, with all her heart, that the moment would never end.

Twelve

By the time they returned to Gracehall, the dinner table was filled with food. Judge Ragsdale offered the blessing.

"Lord, bless this food to our use, and ourselves to Thy service. We thank Thee for this bounty, we thank Thee for the opportunity to gather with friends, old and new. In Christ's name we pray."

A large baked hen anchored one end of the table and a honey-glazed ham the other. In between were all the ingredients needed to make a Christmas dinner worthy of the name: dumplings, cornbread dressing, squash, green beans, white peas, corn, applesauce, hot rolls, pecan pie, pumpkin pie, and fruitcake. For the next few minutes there was little sound save the clinking of utensils against china.

"Everything looks so delicious," Madison said. "But I don't think I've ever seen so much food. How are we ever going to eat all of this?"

"I learned a long time ago that if you just take your time eating, you can eat more," the judge advised.

"Mrs. Duncan, how is Dermott doing?" Laura asked.

"Why, he's as full of vinegar as ever," Cynthia said. "To look at him, you'd hardly know that he nearly drowned this morning."

"I'll bet he doesn't try to do another handstand on the waterwheel," Cora said, and the others laughed.

"Don't you worry about that, Cora," Cynthia replied. "I would sit on him before I let him try that again."

After a long, leisurely dinner, which included samples of more than one dessert, the party moved once again into the keeping room.

The Yule log had burned down, but a sliver of it had been carefully salvaged to be used to start the Yule log next year. The fire was once again built up with fresh wood, so that the entire room was bathed in its warm orange glow.

The chestnuts the men had gathered the day before were now roasted in the fire and, after a while, pulled out and distributed. The rest of the evening was spent in quiet conversation until, once again, pallets were laid out for the children. With that, the adults said their good nights and went up to their own rooms.

When they reached their room, T. J. picked up the bed warmer.

"What are you going to do with that?" Madison asked.

"Same thing I did last night. I'm going to warm the bed."

Madison stepped up, leaned into him, then put her hand up against his cheek. "We don't really need a bed warmer, do we? I mean, if we have each other?"

"Do we have each other?"

Madison pulled away from him and walked over to the bed. She turned the covers down, then turned back to face him.

"Yes, we have each other."

"And this other business, this 'problem' we've been facing?" T. J. asked.

"If we put our . . . heads . . . together," she said with a smile, "I think we can work it out. Don't you?"

"I'm sure we can," he replied, happily closing the distance between them.

This time they were not separated by the bed. On the contrary, it was an invitation, and they met in a loving embrace to experience the passion that had been rekindled earlier in the day when they'd kissed on the mountaintop, under the mistletoe.

Thirteen

December 26

T. J. awakened to the sound of a crow's cawing. As he opened his eyes, the sun streamed in through the window, and the room filled with light and warmth. He lay on his back, and Madison was curled up next to him with her head on his shoulder.

He squeezed her once, and she made a contented little purring sound. He kissed her on the forehead.

"Wake up, sleepyhead."

"No, I don't want to." She snuggled even more closely against him. "I want to stay right here, just like this."

"Have you noticed something?" T. J. asked.

"What?"

"Judge Ragsdale didn't come down the hallway waking everyone up this morning."

"Uhm-hmm," Madison murmured. "Very decent of him to let us sleep in, I would say."

T. J. looked at his watch. "It's after nine o'clock! I can't believe he let us sleep this late."

"Nine?" Madison asked. "Oh, my, we'd better get dressed and get downstairs quickly. I'm sure the kids have been awake for a long time. I don't want them bothering anyone."

T. J. got out of bed and walked over to look through the window. "What in the world?"

"What is it?"

"The snow is gone."

"Well, it was beginning to melt a little yesterday, so I'm not surprised."

"No, I mean all of it is gone."

Madison walked over to look through the window.

"Well, look how bright the sun is. I've seen the sun melt snow very quickly," she said. "Especially if it's warm, and it feels like it is."

"I suppose so," T. J. said. "It just seems strange that there isn't even any snow in the shadows."

"Well, I'm just as glad," Madison replied. "We're going home today, and I wouldn't want to drive back down the mountain with snow on the roads."

"Nor would I," T. J. agreed. "Assuming, that is, we can drive at all. If I can't get the car started, we may have to talk someone into taking us into town, or at least to someplace where I can get a signal on the cell phone."

T. J. and Madison dressed, then went downstairs. Expecting to see everyone seated around the breakfast table, they were surprised when they looked into the dining room to find it empty.

"Hello?" T. J. called. "Where is everyone?"

Sylvia came out of the kitchen and into the foyer. Despite the fact that she was wearing an apron, there was a dusting of flour on her dress.

"Good morning," she greeted them. "I'm making fresh biscuits for breakfast. And if you don't mind leftover ham, I thought I would just fry up a couple of pieces for you. How do you like your eggs? Fried soft or hard? Or maybe you would prefer them scrambled?"

"Uh, fried soft," T. J. said. "Where is everyone?"

"Oh, they're all gone. Except for Angus and Cora MacLeod, that is," Sylvia replied. "They waited around for you, so they could take you back to Mercedes."

"The children," Madison said a little anxiously. "Where are the children?"

"All the children are gone as well," Sylvia said. "Except for Emma, of course. She's in the keeping room with Timothy and Christine. You have fine children, Mrs. Carmichael. Emma is quite taken with them."

"Why, thank you. I'm sure you are aware that Emma is Christine's new best friend."

"Well, Emma couldn't ask for a finer friend than Christine. The children have already had their breakfast, but you may go say good morning to them while I'm getting your breakfast ready. Mr. Carmichael wants his eggs soft. How do you want yours?"

"I don't think I want any eggs, but if you have any of that sourwood honey left, I would love that with my biscuits," Madison said.

"Then that's what you shall have," Sylvia replied, going back into the kitchen. "Oh, and there's coffee already on the table."

"Coffee? That sounds good," T. J. said, starting toward the dining room. "You want me to pour you a cup, Madison?"

"Not just yet. I'm going to check on the kids." Madison walked toward the keeping room.

Timmy, Christine, and Emma were sitting on the floor in front of the fireplace playing pickup sticks. It was apparently Emma's turn, because she was busily picking up the sticks while Timmy kept an eye on the proceedings.

"Good morning," Madison said.

Christine hopped up and ran over to embrace her mother. "Good morning, Mama. Boy, you and Daddy slept a long, long, long time."

"We sure did." Madison returned her daughter's embrace. "Did you two sleep well?"

"I did."

"Dermott and everybody else went home," Timmy said. He didn't take his gaze away from the pile of sticks.

"So I see. You did tell Dermott good-bye, I hope?"

Timmy shook his head. "I couldn't. They were all gone when we woke up this morning."

"You mean you didn't even wake up when everyone left?"

"Nope."

"Well, I'm glad you had a good sleep. It means we are all well rested for the drive back home."

"That stick moved!" Timmy pointed out to Emma, who without argument relinquished her turn.

"I see you're enjoying a game of pickup sticks," Madison said.

"Yes, ma'am, but that's not what they call it here," Timmy said. "They call it jackstraws. Isn't that a funny name for pickup sticks?"

"It's a funny name, all right. Are you kids about ready to go? We're going to start back home right after Daddy and I have our breakfast."

"Okay," Timmy said.

"Mama, can Emma come visit us sometime?" Christine asked.

"I can't come," Emma said.

"Sure you can. If my mama talks to your mama, I'll bet she'll let you come visit me," Christine said.

"No. I can never go where you live," Emma said. "None of us can."

"Mama, go talk to Emma's mama and see if she'll let her come."

"No, sweetheart, Emma is right. She can't come where we live."

"Why not?"

"Because where we live is very . . . different from here. I don't think Emma would care much for it. You remember, don't you, when you wanted to make a pet of that squirrel?"

"Yes, ma'am."

"What happened?"

"I had to let the squirrel go."

"Uh, huh, and do you remember why?"

"Because the squirrel wasn't happy."

"Right. And he wasn't happy because where you brought him was so different from where he lived. If you hadn't let him go, he might have died. Do you remember that?"

"Yes."

"Well, it's like that for Emma. There is just too much of a difference between her world and ours."

"Do you mean Emma might die if she came to visit us?" Christine asked in alarm.

"Well, no, I don't mean to say she would die," Madison

corrected quickly, to make certain that Christine didn't mis-understand her. "But she would be awfully unhappy."

"Sweetheart, breakfast is on the table," T. J. said, coming into the room.

"I'll be right there."

"Mom! Dad called you sweetheart." Timmy smiled broadly. "He hasn't called you sweetheart in a long time."

"That's true," T. J. said, putting his forefinger under Madison's chin and lifting her lips to his for a little kiss. "But I promise you, it won't be a long time before I call her sweetheart again."

"That means I got my Christmas wish, doesn't it?" Timmy said happily.

"Yes, honey, it means you got your Christmas wish," Madison said before she walked away.

"Hooray!" Timmy cheered.

"What Christmas wish is that?" T. J. asked as he and Madison walked to the dining room.

"I'll tell you sometime," Madison answered, putting her arm through his.

T. J. set the luggage down in the foyer, just in front of the door.

John and Sylvia Ragsdale joined them there. "I'm so glad you could spend Christmas with us," the judge said. "I hope you found it enjoyable."

"Enjoyable?" T. J. replied. "Judge Ragsdale, this has been the most memorable Christmas of my entire life. I still want to pay you, though."

"Nonsense. I told you when you arrived that you were my guests. My very special guests."

"Well, I don't know how to thank you."

"Just realizing that you two have worked everything out between you is all the thanks I need."

T. J.'s jaw slackened. "What do you mean?"

"I mean, you are no longer moving apart."

"No, we're not. But how did you know that we were ever having troubles in the first place?"

"Oh, that doesn't matter. What matters is that you have discovered that your love is as strong as it ever was. And you have decided to start attending church again, which will be a wonderful thing for helping you keep your marriage together."

"All right now, Judge, you are beginning to freak me out. How do you know so much about us?"

But the judge just gave them a cryptic smile. "What is important is that you were here, at the right time and place, to save young Dermott Duncan's life, to strengthen your marriage, and to find salvation for your soul. It was all God's plan. They do say God works in mysterious ways, His wonders to perform."

"Yes, Mr. Ragsdale," Madison began, "but—"

"Oh, I see that Angus has brought his carriage around," the judge interrupted, pulling the curtain aside to look through the narrow vertical windowpane that paralleled the front door. "He will take you back to where he found you."

"Oh, by the way, I meant to ask you. Is there someplace nearby where I can get a mechanic?"

"You won't need a mechanic."

"I sure can't repair it. It's all I can do to change a tire."

"Have a little faith, my boy," Judge Ragsdale said. "Have you not seen God work His miracles these last two days? All will be well."

"Judge, as they sometimes say in my business, from your lips to God's ear," T. J. said.

Ragsdale smiled. "Now you understand," he said. "And remember: through God, all things are possible."

"All right, I'm going to hold you to that." T. J. called into the keeping room for Timmy and Christine. "Come on, kids! It's time for us to go!"

"I'll help you with the luggage," the judge said, reaching down to pick up a couple of the suitcases. T. J. got the other two, and they went out front to the carriage, which was sitting in the circular driveway in front of the house. Madison and Sylvia Ragsdale stood there already.

"It has certainly turned into a beautiful day," Madison said.

As Timmy and Christine climbed into the carriage, Madison noticed that she didn't have her doll with her.

"Oh, Christine, have you forgotten the beautiful doll you got for Christmas?"

"I didn't forget, Mama. I gave her to Emma."

"You did?"

"Yes, ma'am. Emma broke the face on her doll, so I gave her Britney. Is that all right?"

Madison walked over to Emma and hugged her. "Of course it's all right. It is more than all right. It is very sweet of you to do that."

"I've got lots and lots of Barbie dolls, but Emma doesn't have any, so I thought it would be okay."

"It's very much okay."

T. J. helped Madison into the carriage, then he climbed in behind her. As the carriage pulled away, they turned to wave good-bye to the Ragsdales, but John and Sylvia were no longer standing on the front porch.

"They sure went back inside in a hurry," Madison commented.

T. J. said, "Well, if you had just had a house full of guests for two days, wouldn't you be about ready for some downtime?"

"Yes, I believe I would." She put her arm through T. J.'s arm. "I love you, Timothy Jerome."

"And I love you, Madison Elaine."

When they reached the car, it was still sitting on the side of the road, exactly as they had left it.

"Well, at least it hasn't been vandalized," T. J. said, as the carriage drew even with the car.

"Did you think it would be?" she asked.

"I was a little concerned, yes."

The carriage stopped just in front of the car.

"Mr. MacLeod, I can't thank you enough for all you have done for us this last couple of days," T. J. said. "You were literally a lifesaver."

Angus nodded, but said nothing in return.

"Madison, would you get that suitcase? Timmy, you get that one, and I'll get these two."

"What should I get, Daddy?" Christine asked.

"You can bring the toys."

After they climbed down from the carriage, T. J. pointed his key ring remote toward the car and clicked it. The trunk opened.

"Hey!" he said happily. "How about that? Maybe the judge was right. Maybe everything is working."

T. J. and the others walked around behind the car to load the suitcase and packages into the trunk. They couldn't see the carriage, because the open trunk blocked their view.

"Mr. MacLeod, don't leave until I'm sure I can get the car started," T. J. called out. He slammed the trunk. "I wouldn't want to . . ."

The carriage was gone.

"What in the world?" T. J. said, looking around. "Madison, did you see him leave?"

"No, I didn't. Where could he have gone this quickly?"

"I don't know, unless there's a turnoff just ahead."

"What are we going to do?"

"Well, if I can get the car started, it doesn't matter."

"Do you think you can?"

"The fact that the remote worked to open the trunk gives me hope." T. J. pointed the remote at the doors, and once more it worked, unlocking all four doors.

T. J. slid behind the wheel and put the key in the ignition. "Christine, say a little prayer for us," he said.

"Dear Lord, please let Daddy get the car started," Christine prayed.

"That ought to do it," T. J. said as he turned the key. The car started instantly.

"Hooray!" they all cheered.

"Christine, from now on you are our go-to person for designated prayer," T. J. said.

"T. J., look—the GPS is working," Madison said.

T. J. glanced at his cell phone. "And so is the cell. I see that I have a message from Evan." He picked up the phone and started to punch in a number. Halfway through he stopped and turned off the phone.

"What's wrong?" Madison asked.

T. J. smiled at her. "Nothing is wrong," he said. "Whatever message Evan has for me can wait."

Madison kissed him.

"Buckle in, kids. We're going home."

"T. J., let's drive back up to Gracehall for a minute."

"Why, did you forget something?"

"No, I'm just curious to see the house one last time."

T. J. turned the car around and started back down the road. Very quickly, they reached County Road 4, then started up the road toward Gracehall.

"Are you sure this is the right road?" Madison asked.

"Yes, I'm sure. The sign said County Road 4."

"It doesn't look the same."

T. J. looked around. "No, it doesn't, does it? For one thing, I don't remember those power lines."

"And look at that house over there. It has a satellite dish."

"Well, it's a cinch they don't belong to Judge Ragsdale's group. We probably just missed it before. After all, we were worried about the car."

"That's true. And, I do remember this turn. The house will be right—"

T. J. slammed on the brakes so hard that the car skidded to a stop.

"T. J.!" Madison gasped. Her voice was a cross between shock and fear.

"I don't understand this," T. J. said. Like Madison's, T. J.'s voice reflected awe and confusion.

T. J. turned the ignition off, and they sat there, staring through the windshield.

The house in front of them was Gracehall. That was obvious by the Corinthian columns, the curved driveway, the gables and cupolas with which they had become so familiar over the past two days. The mill house and waterwheel further identified the property.

But there the similarity ended. The house they were looking at had not seen a paintbrush in years. Most of the windows were boarded over, and those that were not showed broken panes of nearly opaque glass. Loose boards hung from the porch ceiling.

The mill house was even worse. Half its roof was missing. Only about half of the waterwheel was intact, and it had fallen from its axle and was tipped over against the plume. The millpond had dried up.

"Mama, Daddy, what happened to the house?" Christine asked.

"I don't know, darling. As God is in heaven, I don't know."

T. J. opened the door, and the key-in-the-ignition warning began dinging.

"T. J., what are you doing?"

"I'm going to have a look inside."

Madison reached for him. "No, darling, please don't. Let's get out of here."

"Madison, you know there's a logical explanation for this. There has to be."

"If there is, let's find it somewhere else. T. J., this place is giving me goose bumps."

"All right," he said, closing the door. The dinging stopped. "Wait a minute, the cell phone is working now. Give me the Christmas Past brochure. I'm going to call that number again."

"Call them while you're driving," Madison said. "I want to get out of here."

"All right." T. J. started the car. Using the circular driveway, which was still there but overgrown with weeds, he turned the car around and started back.

Madison opened the glove compartment and looked inside. "Did you move the brochure?"

"No."

"It isn't here."

"Look in the console."

Madison opened the console and moved things around as she looked.

"Not here."

Madison had Timmy look around in the backseat, but he also came up empty-handed.

"What's the name of that town that's closest to here?" T. J. asked.

"Possum Hollow?"

"Right. Okay, let's go there."

"Where will you go, to the police? 'Excuse me officer, but my family and I just spent Christmas in a house that looks like nobody has been in it for a hundred years?'"

"No, not the police."

"Where then?"

"We'll start at the library."

Fourteen

The "Welcome to Possum Hollow" sign listed the population as 2,412. Several churches had their names and addresses on the same sign, as did a few civic organizations. It was an attractive town, with broad, tree-lined streets, stately homes, and a thriving downtown area complete with half a dozen recognizable fast-food restaurants, service stations, stores, banks, and lawyers' offices.

They drove by a high school with a sign out front that proudly proclaimed "Possum Hollow High School, Home of the Fighting Possums, 2002 Regional Champions, 2A Basketball."

Two blocks beyond the school, they saw the public library.

"Just what I was looking for," T. J. said. He pulled into the parking lot and stopped. "All right," he said, "let's get some answers."

The library was very much like small-town libraries everywhere, perfumed with the slightly musty aroma of thousands of shelved books and awash in mote-filled sunbeams that splashed in through the high, cloudy, windows. It had wide-plank floors and three long reading tables. Its connection to the twenty-first century was evidenced by the three computer stations.

An attractive woman with short gray hair sat behind a U-shaped counter just inside the door. The name tag on her blazer read "Mrs. Norman." She looked up and smiled a greeting at T. J. and the others as they approached her desk.

"It's always nice to see an entire family visit the library," she said. "May I help you find a book?"

"No, ma'am, but you might be able to give us some information," T. J. said.

"I'll try."

"Mrs. Norman, are you familiar with a house called Gracehall?"

"Yes, of course. It's the Ragsdale house."

T. J. smiled and looked over at Madison. "Well, that's a relief. I was beginning to think that we had lost our minds."

"Is there an Amishlike community nearby?" Madison asked.

"Amish?"

"Yes, you know, people who still live as if they are in the nineteenth century."

"Oh, I know who the Amish are, but there is no Amish community here."

"Well, they aren't actually Amish. They just live as the Amish do."

Mrs. Norman knitted her brow. "I don't know of any group like that around here."

"Well, then, is there a group of reenactors, someone who might re-create Christmases of the past?" T. J. asked.

Again Mrs. Norman shook her head. "I've never heard of such a thing. Why are you asking?"

"We've just come through a very interesting Christmas experience," he replied, "and I think we are beginning to let our imaginations run away with us."

"We didn't imagine Gracehall," Madison interjected.

"Oh, you visited Gracehall?" Mrs. Norman asked.

"Yes."

"Well, Gracehall would certainly be an appropriate place to visit at Christmas."

"Oh? Why is that?"

"They say that Judge Ragsdale's Christmas parties were the biggest thing in the county. Each year he invited a houseful of guests to spend Christmas with his family. It is said that he took great delight in playing Saint Nicholas for all the children, providing all of their gifts at his own expense."

"Yes, that's it!" Madison said. "We just spent Christmas with Judge Ragsdale and his family."

"Oh, I hardly think that is possible," Mrs. Norman said, chuckling. "Judge Ragsdale has been dead for over a hundred years."

"Oh!" Madison gasped. She squeezed T. J.'s arm.

"We have put the judge's house on the National Registry for Historical Homes. The historical society is trying to raise money for its renovation. It will be as beautiful as it ever was when we're finished."

"Oh, well, then that explains everything," T. J. said. "They're using another house like Gracehall as a bed-and-breakfast, and someone is portraying Judge Ragsdale."

"No, that can't be it, T. J. We went back to Gracehall, and it was all run down."

"That wasn't the same road," T. J. said. "You said yourself that it looked different. The historical society must have created a replica of Gracehall as a means of raising money."

Mrs. Norman said, "Oh, no, there's nothing like that. And

I would know, because I'm secretary of the historical society. But we are selling cookbooks to raise money for the restoration." She pointed to a display of books on the counter to her left. "Would you like to buy one?"

"What? Yes, I'll buy one," T. J. responded distractedly.

While T. J. and Madison were talking to Mrs. Norman, Timmy and Christine had been looking around the library. Now Christine came running back.

"Mama, come look!"

Madison and T. J. followed Christine over to a glass display case. Inside were several artifacts, all neatly labeled: photographs, a pair of glasses, a brooch-watch, several books, and a doll. It was the doll that had caught Christine's attention.

"Mama, it's Britney," she said, pointing.

"It does look like Britney, but it couldn't be, honey. Look how old that doll is. There are little crack lines all through her face. Britney didn't have those."

"It is Britney," Christine insisted.

"Madison," T. J. said quietly. "Look at the name on that school." He was pointing to a photograph in the case. The sign on the building in question read "Emma P. Ragsdale Elementary School."

"Oh, that is our tribute to Miss Emma." Mrs. Norman had joined them at the display case. "Possum Hollow is very proud of her. She was a wonderful teacher who got all sorts of national recognition for excellence. In fact, she was my teacher when I was in the fifth grade."

"Miss Emma?" Madison said, astounded.

"Yes. Oh, I know, it probably sounds funny to call an old lady Miss Emma, but she never married, and that's just the way people do it around here. Except her students, of course—we called her Miss Ragsdale. Funny you should be asking about Gracehall, Miss Emma was the last one who actually lived there. But since she died, oh, thirty years ago now, nobody has lived in Gracehall. That's why it got to be so run down."

"You are saying this woman, this Miss Emma who died over thirty years ago, was the daughter of John and Sylvia Ragsdale?"

"Yes."

T. J. looked puzzled, angry. "If what you are saying is true, then I think my family and I have been the victims of a very elaborate hoax."

"That's what it has to be," Madison averred. "But they didn't ask for money. And we had a wonderful experience. It makes you wonder why they would have gone to such trouble."

"Mrs. Norman, do you have any pictures of Judge Ragsdale?" T. J. asked.

"Well, yes, as a matter of fact, we do." She went into the back of the library and began rummaging through a file folder.

"T. J., do you really think this was all some kind of practical joke?" Madison asked.

"What else could it be?" he replied.

Mrs. Norman returned with a manila folder. "We have several pictures. Here's one of the judge with his second wife, Emma's mother." She removed the picture from the folder and handed it to them. Just then the telephone rang, and she excused herself to answer the call.

The photograph was typical of many such portraits taken

at the end of the nineteenth century. It showed a man sitting stiffly in a chair, with a woman standing beside him, her hand on his shoulder, both gazing formally at the camera.

"T. J., look!" Madison pointed to a brooch on the woman's blouse. It was a golden treble clef with a small stone inset.

"It's them!" T. J. gasped. "It's really them!" He turned the picture over. The inscription on back read "Judge John and Mrs. Sylvia Ragsdale, Christmas, 1893."

"T. J., this can't mean what I think it means, can it?"

"You mean, did we somehow go back to 1893?"

Madison's nose crinkled incredulously. "It just isn't possible."

"Wait, I want to check something."

He led Madison back over to Mrs. Norman's desk, just as she was hanging up the phone. She looked up at them with a broad smile. "Did the photograph help you any?"

"Yes," he answered. "Mrs. Norman, are your computers connected to the Internet?"

"Oh yes, of course."

"I wonder if I could use one of them."

"Why, certainly. Those three are here for the use of our patrons," she said, gesturing. "Number three is already logged on. Help yourself."

"Thank you."

"What are you going to do?" Madison asked, as T. J. sat down at the computer.

"Last night, and the night before, the moon was full, right?" He typed in some words and clicked.

"Yes."

"I'm doing a search for lunar phases. There must be a site

that will show them for every year." The screen came up, and T. J. glanced over the results. He selected an address and clicked on it. When the site came up, he clicked on the current date. "Look at the moon phase for last night and the night before," he said.

"Why, it's just a sliver."

T. J. clicked on December 24, 1893. "Now look."

Madison gasped. "No. It can't be!"

The moon phase was full.

As they drove west on I-40, returning to Nashville, the entire family rode in silence, trying to grasp what they had just experienced.

"Hey, kids, I'm going to call Grandma and put her on the speaker," T. J. said, breaking the long silence. "You can tell her we had a nice Christmas, but don't say anything about all the rest of it, okay?"

"Why not?" Christine asked.

"I think that what just happened to us . . . whatever it was . . . was just for us," T. J. said.

"I agree," Madison said.

"I'm not going to tell anyone," Timmy said. "If I did, they'd think I was nuts."

Madison laughed. "Yes, there is that to consider."

T. J. dialed his mother's number, and the phone rang through the car speaker.

"Hello?"

"Hello, Mom," T. J. said. "We're on our way back home, and I just thought I would report in and let everyone say hi."

Madison, Timmy, and Christine exchanged Christmas greetings with T. J.'s mother, and then she asked where they had spent Christmas.

"We were in the mountains, not too far from Crossville, near a little town called Possum Hollow."

"Did you say Possum Hollow?"

"Yes."

"Well, now, that is an interesting coincidence."

"What do you mean?"

"Your grandmother was born in Possum Hollow."

"What? I thought Grandma was from Chattanooga."

"Well, she was. But my grandparents were on a train coming back from a visit to St. Louis when my grandmother went into labor with Mama. They had to leave the train at Possum Hollow and find a doctor. It was a good thing they did, too, because the baby almost died."

"Wait a minute," T. J. protested. "Why haven't I heard this piece of family history before?"

"Well, it's not the sort of thing that comes up every day," his mother replied. "I haven't thought about it in years."

"So what was wrong with Grandma?"

"She wasn't breathing. My grandma said that the doctor started breathing in the baby's mouth right away and saved her life."

"Breathing into her mouth? I didn't know they knew CPR in those days."

"Well, I just know what she told me. If you want the whole

story, you can read the personal memoirs Mama wrote several years before she died. I'm sure it's all in there."

"Mom, do me a favor, would you? Could you look it up now, and see what other details she tells?"

"Right now? Well, all right, but it may take a few minutes. I hate for you to use up so much time on your car phone."

"I've got plenty of time," T. J. said.

In a moment she was back on the line. "There really isn't any more than what I've already told you . . . except that she tells the name of the doctor . . . it looks like Dement, no . . . Dermott, that's what it is. Dr. Dermott Duncan of Possum Hollow."

T. J. felt goose bumps, and he looked over at Madison. The reaction in her face mirrored his own.

"T. J., are you still there? Did we lose the signal?"

"I'm still here, Mom," T. J. said.

"I wondered, you were so quiet for a moment."

"I know. Listen, I'd better pay attention to what I'm doing here. We'll stop by to see you before we get home."

"Okay, you drive carefully now."

"I will. Good-bye."

"Good-bye."

They rode along quietly for another moment. "Madison, do you realize that if we hadn't done what we did, if Dermott had died, I might not even be here now?"

"Yes," Madison replied in a barely audible voice.

"He knew."

"Who knew what?"

"Judge Ragsdale knew our names. He knew about our

problem when we arrived. And he knew that we had it settled before we left."

"But how could he have known?"

"As he said, this whole thing was God's plan. The judge was merely an instrument of that plan."

Madison reached across the console and gave T. J.'s hand a squeeze.

He squeezed back. "It really gives meaning to the part of our marriage vows where it says, 'Whom God hath put together, let no man put asunder.'"

Madison looked at him, seeing something, someone different. "It gives us an awesome responsibility to make sure this works, doesn't it?"

"Yes, it does," T. J. agreed. "And we will make it work. Do you want to know how I know?"

"How?"

"Because my mind keeps going back to something Judge Ragsdale said to us just before we left."

"What was that?"

"Through God, all things are possible."

"I've no doubt of that. But I just wonder why He chose us. . . ."

"Because, I asked Him to," Timmy said as he flipped the ball into the wooden cup in his hand.

About the Author

Robert Vaughan is the author of more than 250 published works including *Andersonville*, which was made into the popular TNT television miniseries. A retired military officer, Vaughan and his wife, Ruth, live in Gulf Shores, Alabama.

PRAISE FOR ROBERT VAUGHAN:

"Robert Vaughan knows war, love, and the Lord . . . you just want more."

—Oliver North,
former U.S. Marine and host of the nationally syndicated program "Common Sense Radio with Oliver North"

"[Vaughan] blends accurate history with colorful fiction. First-rate writing that entertains and instructs."

—Gilbert Morris,
bestselling novelist and teacher

His Truth Is Marching On:
A WWII Novel

Dewey Bradley wants nothing more than to graduate from college, marry his girlfriend Unity, and become a pastor of a church. But when war breaks out, Dewey—impassioned by the atrocities of the Nazis—drops out of school to enlist. Meanwhile, Gunter Reinhardt is forced to leave engineering school and join the German army. The two unknowingly cross paths as enemies on several occasions. While Dewey's heart is hardened by the brutality of war, Gunter becomes disillusioned with Hitler and his country. In a critical moment, Dewey and Gunter come face-to-face. One will choose to spare the life of the other, and in doing so, will ultimately spare his own soul.

ISBN: 0-7852-6185-0

In the three books of this series, Robert Vaughan utilizes his own war experiences to weave stories of intrigue and passion, offering readers a suspenseful look at WWII.